W9-AHQ-981

TRINITY
TRINITY
TRINITY

TRINITY
TRINITY
TRINITY

A NOVEL

BY ERIKA KOBAYASHI

TRANSLATED FROM THE JAPANESE
BY BRIAN BERGSTROM

ASTRA HOUSE NEW YORK

Originally published in the Japanese language as
Trinity, Trinity, Trinity (トリニティ、トリニティ、トリニティ)

Astra House
A Division of Astra Publishing House
astrahouse.com

Printed in the United States of America

Library of Congress Cataloging-in-Publication Data

Names: Kobayashi, Erika, 1978– author. | Bergstrom, Brian, translator.
Title: Trinity, trinity, trinity : a novel / by Erika Kobayashi ;
translated from the Japanese by Brian Bergstrom.
Other titles: Torinito, torinito, torinito. English
Description: First edition. | New York : Astra House, 2022. | Includes bibliographical references. | Summary: "Trinity, Trinity, Trinity is a novel set in a world in which Japanese senior citizens display symptoms of a mysterious condition known as "Trinity," about a woman who suspects her mother has been drawn into a terrorist attack, and sets out to uncover family secrets, finding unexpected connections between the Olympics and Japan's history of atomic power"—Provided by publisher.
Identifiers: LCCN 2022000448 (print) | LCCN 2022000449 (ebook) |
ISBN 9781662601156 (hardcover) | ISBN 9781662601163 (epub)
Subjects: LCGFT: Thrillers (Fiction) | Novels.
Classification: LCC PL872.5.O245 (print) | LCC PL872.5.O245 (ebook) |
DDC 895.63/6—dc23/eng/20220113
LC record available at https://lccn.loc.gov/2022000448
LC ebook record available at https://lccn.loc.gov/2022000449

First edition

10 9 8 7 6 5 4 3 2 1

Design by Richard Oriolo
The text is set in Arno Pro.
The titles are set in BN Tillsdale.

CONTENTS

TRINITY

TRINITY

TRINITY

PROLOGUE

Lately, even when it's light outside, I find I can't tell if it's morning or evening, if the sun is coming up or on its way back down. When I force my eyelids apart to check, all I see is a wide plane of sky the color of burning.

I blink, and blink again.

Looking over from my pillow, I catch sight of a clock.

5:23

The numbers stand out clearly on its display.

The clock is cheap, plastic. The crocheted lace doily lying beneath it is more to my liking, a pineapple motif woven into its pattern.

I try to lift my hand to trace the pineapple with my finger.

But it's heavy as lead.

And not just my hand, my whole body is heavy, encased in lead.

Lead.

It doesn't feel like a metaphor. It feels literal, as if now I know the exact feeling of lead being poured over my whole body.

Still, I feel as though touching the lace would unlock something—would allow me to remember more than I do. I concentrate my energy into my hand. My fingers brush against something; it feels like a remote control of some sort. I grab it and notice trailing down from it a thick cord.

What does it connect to?

There's an orange bump in its center. Some sort of button?

My hand slowly grips the control, and I use all my might to push the button.

A sudden rumbling begins, accompanied by shaking.

The ground begins to shift beneath me. The shaking sounds like the growl of a beast.

My eyes fly open, as does my mouth, as I try to scream a scream that refuses to come out.

But it's not the ground that's shifting.

It's the bed. The section beneath my back and the section beneath my legs are rising at the same time.

Startled, I throw the controller away. The rumbling abates; the shaking subsides.

I look around.

All that's visible through the window is sky.

Where is this place? Who am I?

I seem to have forgotten.

I seem to have been asleep for quite a long time.

It also seems like quite a long time since I woke up.

White tissue paper sticking up from the box on the round table next to the bed flutters in the breeze from the air conditioner.

The flooring in the room strikes me as too white. The walls are unpleasantly white as well, spreading out in all directions, yet also flimsy, as if nothing more than papier-mâché.

I search the walls for paintings.

Where's the Cézanne?

The Maurice de Vlaminck?

And of course—the Van Gogh! *Enclosed Field with Rising Sun* should be right over there!

The golden orb in the sky. The valleys dividing the blue mountains. The field dyed gold by the sun's rays. The brick-red roof of the small cottage at the foot of the mountains, the three cedars clustered nearby. The grooves and ridges of the paint itself. The delicate touches left by fine-pointed brushstrokes.

I remember it so vividly—every nook and cranny of that painting.

And the room it hung in as well. The patterns of the sofa cushions, the exact shape of every knickknack decorating the mantelpiece—I can remember it all, everything about it, down to the last detail.

It's New York, Manhattan, Riverside Drive. Robert Oppenheimer's house.

I blink again, then again and again, staring at the wall in front of me.

But the view remains the same: an expanse of embossed wallpaper. No plaster.

I somehow will my body to move. My feet touch the floor.

My toenails touch the slick floor.

I look down at them and recoil in horror.

My nails are yellow and cracked, powdery and brittle.

What is the meaning of this? How did I end up in such miserable shape?

I'm dressed in pajamas made of light-blue sweatshirt material, top and bottom. They're covered in pilling. And are the cuffs of the pants elastic? Where's the elegant negligee I should be wearing? Though now I can't seem to remember so clearly—would it have been the one with the exquisite round buttons or the one that closed with satin ribbon?

The chill breeze from the air conditioner reaches my bare feet.

From the corner of my eye, I catch a glimpse of a claw-footed mahogany chest. A black, cylindrical object rests atop it. It reminds me of a monolith—yet, also, of something altogether different. The lace beneath is tatted in a geometric crisscross pattern I find quite chic.

I move in for a closer look.

I focus my energy into both legs. Feet planted on the floor, I raise myself off the edge of the bed. I'm standing!

Gravity seems to pull my entire body down.

I take a step.

I stagger as I do, but manage to regain my balance.

One step, then another. I reach my hands out. Only a little farther and I can touch it!

But at that very moment, my legs buckle and my hands fly into the air.

I've fallen.

I've fallen right down onto the floor.

The back of my head hurts so much it feels like it's splitting open.

The ceiling, as too-white as the rest of the room, swims into view. It seems to be slowly moving.

A moan escapes my lips. I turn over so I'm lying on my side.

I feel something warm and touch my hand to my head; my fingers come away slick with red. I feel a scream building within me. Blood. It's blood.

I hurriedly wipe the blood on my pajama bottoms, near the crotch.

As I writhe around on the floor, I notice another black object sitting there before my eyes.

I touch its shiny black surface and it lights up. An LCD screen!

A triangular shape appears in its center. I tap it.

Music begins to play. It's earsplittingly loud.

"Sunrise Serenade " by Glenn Miller and His Orchestra.

I hear trumpet, trombone, piano—it's the Big Band sound.

I hum along with the melody.

This is the record's A-side. The B-side, I know, is "Moonlight Serenade." A song so famous you hear it playing at cafés and supermarkets. Yet, I can't remember how it goes, such a well-known song.

"Sunrise Serenade" is reaching its crescendo.

That's right, this was the song that came on the radio that day, right after the end of *The Skypilot*.

The countdown: 10, 9, 8, 7, 6 . . .

I raise my head after counting down that far and something warm slides down my forehead and drips off my face. Red stains appear on the chest of my light-blue pajama top.

Blood. It's blood. I don't really know why, but I start wiping my forehead with my hand. I wipe again and again but to no avail, the blood just keeps flowing. I wipe furiously with my hands, trying to remove it. Blood stains spread across the floor beneath me. Still wiping, I slowly look up.

The door to the room is opening.

A girl stands in the doorway, alone.

She looks to be around thirteen or fourteen. She's gripping another blackly shiny object in one hand. Her eyes are a dark, rich color, framed by long lashes. Her hair's been cut too short in both the back and front, making it stick up in places.

The girl's eyes widen into saucers.

"Grandma, are you okay?"

She runs to me as she shouts her question.

She's wearing a black T-shirt that strikes me as unsuitable to wear outside the house, with large white lettering spelling DEATH BE NOT PROUD running across the chest, over her small breasts. As she kneels beside me, her firm, pants-less thighs emerge from beneath it, exposed.

Surprised, I scoot away from her as best I can while lying on my side.

Still, I see as she gets closer that she has lace around her middle—picot lace, to be exact.

The girl turns away from me and her thin lips part to allow her to scream toward the door.

"Come here! Mom! Quick!"

Her voice is loud enough to drown out the song I'd been listening to so intently. She snatches the shiny black object from my hand and suddenly the music stops.

The song—

The song had almost reached the best part!

Just a little longer and something, not just in the song but something else too—it had all been on the verge of starting.

The light shining in the girl's hand disappears. Darkness appears in its place.

I peer into that darkness.

The girl peers at me.

"Grandma, don't worry, they're coming, it won't be long."

Behind her, in the window, the sun continues to look as if it were both coming up and going down.

By the way, I think, *I've been meaning to ask—you keep saying Grandma, Grandma, but tell me: who is "Grandma"?*

I look behind me to see if someone is standing there.

Grandma?

But there's no one there, no one behind me at all, and so it must be me, I'm the one she must be calling "Grandma"!

Grandma.

I look at the girl straight on.

This girl—she's mine? And not even my daughter, but my granddaughter?

The girl is running her finger across a shiny black object, a different one than the one she took from me. The LCD screen lights up, illuminating her face with its glow.

There's a sticker on the back of it with the same slogan as her shirt: DEATH BE NOT PROUD.

I recognize the poem. I remember another of his clearly enough to recite it.

Batter my heart, three-person'd God; for you
As yet but knock; breathe, shine, and seek to mend;
That I may rise and stand, o'erthrow me, and bend
Your force to break, blow, burn, and make me new.

The girl brings the shiny black object to her ear.

"Hello?"

The object pressed to her ear looks like a shiny black stone.

"Yes.

"She hit her head, she's bleeding.

"Yes.

"She's conscious."

I narrow my eyes as I watch her.

Who is this girl?

If I'm supposed to be her *grandma,* that means I must have given birth to either her mother or father.

I try my hardest to remember, but nothing comes up.

The girl finishes her conversation and then bends down, grips me by the waistband of my pajama pants, and lifts me up.

I try to stand but end up falling on my knees, and I notice the crotch of my pajama bottoms is soaked in blood. Is it my period?

All I remember is a dull, heavy feeling in my lower body.

I cling to the girl's body and finally manage to pull myself up.

My fingers touch the lace at her middle.

1, 2, 3, 4, 5

1, 2, 3, 4, 5

Crochet hooks are moving in my head. A white ball of lace yarn rotates where it sits on my knee.

1, 2, 3, 4, 5

1, 2, 3, 4, 5

A thread becomes a loop, and then a loop hooks to another loop, and then another, and forms a pattern. That's right—I was going to crochet some lace!

1, 2, 3, 4, 5

1, 2, 3, 4, 5

But the pattern I was weaving went wrong somewhere, I must have made a mistake along the way.

I try to move my feet and end up dragging them heavily across the floor.

The room is darkening all around me.

I need to turn on the light.

I reach up with both hands, searching for the string to pull. But the lights in this room don't have strings hanging from them, and suddenly—

Hey!

I find myself shouting at the black cylinder for some reason, and then darkness swallows me as I collapse again.

Darkness.

I HEAR THE sound of a door opening and shutting.

I hear the sound of footsteps loudly approaching.

I hear the sound of women talking to each other in hushed tones.

And then I hear the sound of one of the women leaning close to my ear and shouting:

"Mother, are you okay?!"

She called me *Mother*—does that mean this is my daughter's voice?

"Mother?"

A different woman's voice this time, quavering a bit and calling me Mother too.

"We don't have to take her to the hospital, do we? She'll be all right, right?"

So I have not one daughter, but two?

The first woman snorts in response to the other.

"She'll be all right."

"She has quite a sense of timing, doesn't she? Taking this moment, right on the day of the Opening Ceremony of the Olympics, to fall down!"

The women are hurriedly moving around my bed.

"What time were they going to stop traffic for the torch relay anyway? Though I guess that wouldn't matter so much for an ambulance . . ."

The sound of footsteps recedes, grows distant.

Quiet returns to the room.

I hear the girl whisper in my ear.

"Can you hear it?"

Slowly, I open my eyes.

I can't tell if it's morning or evening, if the sun is coming up or on its way back down.

SUNRISE

The geology of the country round here has taken up my attention for some years now. The doctors say that one should not read or write or even think; but perhaps a calm contemplation of nature might still be entertaining and refreshing. Here in Carlsbad, our attention is drawn above all to rocks and stones, the most ancient, the newer and the most recent, some in the depths of the primeval world; others are being formed every day, all leading us from effect to cause, from cause to something higher.

—Johann Wolfgang von Goethe
Letter to Carl Franz Anton Ritter von Schreibers, from Carlsbad
May 23, 1820

8:00

Clear liquid slowly formed into a drop, and then, succumbing to gravity, fell.

My mother looked up at the IV bag connected to her left arm and counted the falling drops.

1, 2, 3, 4, 5

Her lips were the only part of her that moved, except when she would blink from time to time, as if remembering something. Her long eyelashes would flutter as she did.

The dimly lit hospital room was meant for six, and my mother's bed was the furthest from the door, beneath the window. She lay there surrounded by the whiteness of the hospital bed, a netting-covered bandage wrapped around her head and the light-blue sweats she'd been wearing replaced with a hospital-provided pink nightgown.

Trembling, I contemplated my mother as she lay before me, transformed so completely.

How had it come to this?

We had had a home care worker coming during the day for support and were going to the hospital for rehab. We'd even installed new fixtures in the shower. And in fact, her leg had been improving so rapidly it had shocked her nurse, and with help she'd been able to walk to the bathroom herself and move about her room using a crutch.

I wanted to believe this was all a big mistake.

My mother now acted as if nothing around her had anything to do with her, and she seemed unable or unwilling even to look at me.

1, 2, 3, 4, 5

1, 2, 3, 4, 5

She was still counting the drops.

I remembered my mother sitting on a love seat upholstered in deep-green velvet. My mother young, beautiful.

She was wearing a voluminous satin skirt. Her pale legs were long and shapely as they emerged from beneath it. She was crocheting white lace with golden hooks she held in her hands.

On the brushed-plaster wall behind her hung a painting showing a golden sun shining down on a field. It was a page ripped from a calendar of famous paintings and put in a frame, but it looked like a piece of grand art hanging there in this room.

The brass doorknobs, the oak-paneled floors, the china cabinet enclosed in stained glass—everything in the room had been carefully selected by my mother. This house in the Tokyo suburbs, like the 1964 Olympics taking place right then, like my mother herself, dazzled the eye with resplendence.

Same price tag as the Olympics, too—my father would mutter this to himself as a joke.

But my younger sister hated it, this fusty old house with its brass doorknobs and lace doilies on everything. She refused to invite her friends over to see it.

The golden hooks in my mother's hands began to move.

1
2
3
4
5

Her mouth moved in concert with the hooks. Her lips were painted a beautiful red. The white lace yarn slipped steadily through her hands, a single thread transforming in an instant into a complex matrix of loops and stitches to form brilliant patterns. Like a form of magic.

From time to time, my mother would blink, as if remembering something. Her long eyelashes would flutter as she did.

Her dark eyes fixed me with their gaze.

I caught my breath, looking at her.

But none of it existed any longer—not my mother looking like this, not the house itself.

I could see my mother's blood, a cloudy red so dark it was nearly black, as it was sucked briefly back into the tube that connected her pale, vein-patterned arm to the IV drip.

THE TELEVISION ATTACHED to the wall beside her bed was soundlessly showing the Olympic torch relay. It had begun back in the spring and was now finally reaching the site of the Opening Ceremony for the 2020 Tokyo Olympics, and excitement was coming to a head. The screen was filled with images of huge crowds lining both sides of the relay route for a chance to get even a brief glimpse of the torch as it passed, despite the forty-plus-degree heat that had been continuing for days.

The people lining the streets snapped photos with their phones and waved little Japanese flags with red circles in their centers; chyrons ran along the bottom of the screen warning people to keep hydrated and avoid sunstroke. Volunteers dressed in polo shirts checkered in light blue and white could be seen circulating through the crowd. There seemed to be an unusually large amount of security, too, perhaps as a precaution against terrorist attack.

A woman was driving down the middle of the route in an electric wheelchair. Countless police cars and white motorbikes followed in her wake.

I opened my eyes wide as I stared at her on the screen.

Sweat streamed from the woman's forehead, but her expression was one of confidence and joy.

Yes—this is effort, how it should look.

The torch was mounted on the back of the wheelchair, white smoke trailing from the flame that blazed dazzlingly even in the bright morning sun.

It's okay.

I murmured this to myself, my mouth dry, as I stared into the flame.

It's okay.

I made—or rather, we *made—the effort. Mother just got a little hurt, that's all.*

Perhaps because I hadn't gotten a good night's sleep in days, my heart would not stop racing.

The hospital room was so quiet. Cream-colored curtains were drawn tightly around the neighboring beds, making it seem like my mother and I had been left all alone. But maybe everyone else really was there, silently watching the torch relay like we were, hidden from view. Light streamed in the window, the same color as the curtains, and I watched as it spread across their thin cloth, making it glow.

My daughter, sitting in the chair next to the bed, was looking over at the television, too, her mouth fallen half-open.

She was thirteen years old, dressed in a tight-fitting black T-shirt and black jeans, over which, for fashion or some other reason, she had thrown a lace vest my mother had made. She had wireless earbuds in her ears, and I could hear the faint sound of drums leaking from them. The earbuds looked as if they were connected to an unseen device with invisible cords. DEATH BE NOT PROUD: the name of the band she was obsessed with, emblazoned on her shirt. Was that what she was listening to? The shiny black sticker stuck to the case of the phone in her hand bore the same legend: DEATH BE NOT PROUD.

My daughter blinked, slowly.

Her long eyelashes, her dark eyes, her slightly upturned nose—she looked almost exactly like me, and sometimes it felt like I was looking at myself when I looked at her.

Though she had deliberately cut her hair too short, and it stuck up all over seemingly on purpose—did she use hair wax or something? If she'd just grow it out a bit and maybe use a hot curler, she'd look a little more feminine, a little cuter, and would surely be quite popular with the boys. Instead, she wore that beat-up old T-shirt and went around with no make up at all. She didn't seem to care a bit about that sort of thing. Well, maybe it was better than caring too much.

The woman in the wheelchair was still driving herself down the lane, bearing the sacred fire with her.

It was only going to be a few hours before it passed through this neighborhood.

My daughter and my sister were supposed to have joined me to go and watch as it passed. Last night, I'd put Pocari Sweat in the freezer for the big day—preparations that were now in vain.

I decided to break the silence, and turned to my daughter, saying, "It's too bad, isn't it?"

My daughter answered without missing a beat, her eyes still glued to the television. "Not really. We can always catch it sometime later, maybe next time the Olympics come here."

"I guess that's true," I answered, looking down at my mother as she lay in bed.

Sometime. When would that be, exactly? 2044? 2076?

This is what I was thinking about as my sister came in, having gone home to fetch things to help our mother get situated in the hospital. She was wearing white sneakers, her hair pulled back into a severe bun. She had Mother's floral-patterned bag slung over one shoulder, filled to bursting with things for the hospital stay, and a frozen bottle of Pocari Sweat in her hand.

Beads of condensation slid down the bottle to slowly form drops that, eventually, fell to the floor.

"I thought she'd finally kicked the bucket this time," she said, snorting as she looked down at the bed.

I drew up short, shocked. My daughter pulled the earbuds from her ears, murmuring, "Oh my god, you're talking so loud . . ."

My sister threw herself into the round chair on the other side of the bed. Her jersey shirt rode up a bit, exposing flesh that spilled over the waist of her jeans.

"Too bad, we were supposed to be on the other side of the TV screen today . . ."

I glanced back at the television.

Marine Day and Sports Day had both been moved due to the Revised Olympics Special Measures Act, creating a sudden four days off in a row. My sister, who worked at a web production company and couldn't usually take vacation when she wanted, had finally gotten time off for this.

Ice rattled in the half-frozen bottle in her hand.

Fighting my rising sense of unease, I said, in as bright a tone as possible, "Well, I guess I better go to work!"

My sister and daughter just waved, their eyes locked on the television screen.

My chest hurt.

I looked back at my mother in the hospital bed again and again.

But like before, she made no attempt to return my gaze.

Of all the days to have to go to work! It was a nine-to-five job normally, with weekends and holidays off. But recently, we'd advertised an offer to install new water-purification systems for half the price—and with 20 percent off the price of new cartridges!—as a "health support campaign" anticipating the Olympics, and the response had been much greater than we expected. We were a small company, and of the three people heading the campaign, one had gone on maternity leave at the beginning of the month, while the other had done the same starting last week, leaving me to manage everything on my own.

As I walked out into the hall, I turned one last time to look back at my mother in her bed, but the curtains near me blocked her from view.

I slung my black synthetic-leather bag over my shoulder and headed toward the elevators.

I was passing the nurses' station when an old man pushing an IV stand appeared in front of me, heading my way. I gasped and took a step back. I ducked into a nearby restroom to avoid him. As soon as I stepped behind the partition, I saw an LED light go on. I'd apparently tripped some sort of invisible switch. All around me, the air smelled strongly of disinfectant.

My heart was racing again.

All because of that old man.

But for all I knew, he could have been a diabetic patient, or had heart disease—he was in the hospital for some innocent reason like that, surely.

I shouldn't jump to conclusions.

But I hadn't slept well lately and was very tired.

I took a deep breath, then stood in front of the mirror.

I could see dark shadows beneath my eyes. I pulled my organic sunscreen lotion from my purse and began to apply it. I concentrated on trying to conceal the shadows under my eyes and any spots on my cheeks.

Leaving the restroom, I saw the old man was nowhere to be found. I looked all around to make sure he was really gone, then headed toward the elevators once more, at a trot.

In the waiting room on the first floor, there were three people who appeared to be elderly sitting on the yellow vinyl sofa.

One was hard to place in age but seemed to be going bald; the other two had quite a lot of white in their hair and were pretty hunched over. All three seemed to be glancing at one another from their various positions on the sofa, then looking down again as if to confirm they were still holding whatever they might be holding in their hands.

I passed as quickly as I could behind where they were sitting.

I walked by a few middle-aged men and women on my way out past the billing counter.

The huge television monitor mounted on the wall showed the woman in the wheelchair carrying the torch, just like before.

Then it happened, right as I was striding purposefully toward the entrance.

A loud beeping, like an alarm, rang out.

Hearing it, I thought my breath would stop completely.

My heart tightened in my chest.

I turned to look behind me.

A man wearing glasses and a brown checked shirt was moving around, as if in a frenzy, next to the billing counter. He held a ¥10,000 bill in one hand and a Geiger counter in the other. It was the Geiger counter that was beeping so loudly.

I could hear people murmuring to one another. They turned as one to look toward the commotion.

9:00

s soon as the automatic doors of the hospital opened, my ears were filled with the buzz of cicadas. The beeping of the Geiger counter receded behind me as the wet heat outside enveloped my body.

There was a small garden on the far right side of the drop-off area, an expanse of grass split cleanly into sections of light and shadow. Palms and azaleas flourished in the sunlight, while in the shadows, a statue of Mary in white robes with a blue sash stood atop a large stone. A man in a wheelchair and the woman who had been pushing him bent their heads before her, crossing themselves in fervent prayer even in the heat.

Our Lady of Lourdes.

Before I headed toward the sunlit section of the garden, I poured some purified water into my mouth from the silver thermos I carried and slid long black gloves onto both hands, pulling them up to the elbow.

My father's mother had been a Nagasaki-born, fervent Christian. She'd moved to Tokyo at sixteen and neither her Nagasaki accent nor any stories from her past ever escaped her lips; only her faith remained unchanged.

In France, there's a small village called Lourdes. A poor little girl once lived there.

My grandmother would show up at our house on the barest of pretexts and tell us the story of the miracle, an unfiltered Lucky Strike between her fingers and a dead-serious expression on her face.

Her name was Bernadette. She was fourteen years old.

One day, our grandmother would tell us, the Sacred Mother appeared to Bernadette. She pointed to the rocks at the bottom of a nearby cave and told the little girl she must dig. The little girl obeyed, removing the rocks and digging into the earth with her bare hands.

And wouldn't you know it—soon enough, a spring emerged, burbling up from the ground.

The spring was a miracle. A blind man who drank its water could see again. A man who couldn't walk could bathe himself and walk again.

Cigarette smoke would flow from between our grandmother's yellowing teeth as she told her story. Remembering her now, I thought of my mother lying in her hospital bed.

Our grandmother was always serious when she spoke of the miracle.

Everyone who visits the spring leaves cured of what ailed them.

Then she would point at her own bent legs and add, *But it costs money to go there.*

According to her, the miraculous spring flowed even now, and scores of believers made the pilgrimage to its waters. After I became an adult, I looked it up on the internet myself and saw photos of the cavern walls covered in crutches and artificial limbs left behind by believers who were cured there and walked away. It seemed to be a tangible miracle, observable to anyone.

My father didn't believe in miracles and wasn't a Christian, but it was his custom to give his mother a brown envelope of cash when she would visit.

Though it was also his custom to blow on the envelope as he held it out for her, making her truly angry. For when he blew on it, the envelope would disappear.

It was his special magic trick.

He would blow again into thin air and: poof! The envelope would appear somewhere else—in the pocket of a coat hanging on a hanger, in a teacup sitting on the table. Sometimes he would make the envelope burst into flames at the touch of his finger.

If you keep this up, God will surely punish you.

Muttering to herself, my grandmother would check and recheck that the money was still in the envelope as she got ready to leave.

Even so, I never heard that she ever made the trip to Lourdes before she died. Perhaps the entire ritual was just a way to get money, or perhaps she never quite saved up enough for the trip; either way, I wondered if making the trip to Lourdes would have really healed her legs.

In the name of the Father, the Son, and the Holy Ghost. Amen.

In front of me now, the man in the wheelchair and the woman standing behind him were crossing themselves, their eyes shut tight against the hot sun beating down on them as they made their lengthy prayers. The man's cheeks were quite sunken in; he might not have much time left.

Nevertheless, that time might get even shorter if he stayed so long in the heat that he got sunstroke. I put on my sunglasses, opened my silver umbrella, and walked away.

APPROACHING THE TRAIN station, I saw that a big stage had been constructed in the center of the roundabout in front of it. Maybe it was the brightness of the sun, but the neon-pink lights hung around the stage seemed grotesquely flashy to me as I got closer.

Heat was rising in waves from the asphalt already, and it was probably going to get even hotter this afternoon. School had let out for summer, but my daughter's school's symphonic band was scheduled to play the "Tokyo Olympics 2020 Song" at one o'clock. Several of her friends were in the band. Of course, the student welfare committee at the school had kicked up a fuss about the heat and the danger of sunstroke, but it was a once-in-a-lifetime opportunity to perform so close to where the Olympic torch would be passing. So, the decision was made that the show would go on, with a tent set up on stage to shade the children as they played.

In four years
We'll meet again—
And that's a promise!
This is not a dream
Oh yeah, let's go!
This is not a dream
It's the Olympics!
We'll be together, face to face—
Feel the beat—bum-ba-bum, bum-ba-bum!
We'll be together, face to face!

The official "Tokyo Olympics 2020 Song" lyrics were displayed on a huge LCD panel mounted on the side of the station building.

I was facing the stage, using my hands to trace 2-0-2-0 in the air in front of me as I did the little dance with everyone else, when I felt a sudden, dull pain in my stomach. I ran to the restroom inside the station.

The station's air conditioning was blessedly cool even in the restroom, but still I was bathed in sweat. My long black gloves were stuck to my sweaty arms, so I left them on as I pulled my beige, knee-length shapewear panties down and sat on the toilet. There was a dark red bloodstain on the crotch. Counting on my fingers, I realized that my period had arrived right on time, not a day to spare.

Looking at the blood, I found it hard to breathe.

It was like a symbol of all the effort I'd been making in vain, and it chilled me.

What my uterus and ovaries had worked so hard to create over 28 days—672 hours!—all ended up as so much waste. If I'd managed to have sex, conceive, and give birth, it could have been a life.

As despair began to overtake me, my phone vibrated. I bent over, my lower half still exposed, and fished the phone out of my pants pocket so I could peer into it. The face-recognition software opened the phone, the screen unlocking as if by an unseen force. A pop-up notification appeared.

You have a new message from Trinity.

With a bit of trepidation, I used my finger to tap the notification.

The website on the other side of the link filled the screen. After the automatic log-in, a glittering yellow inverted triangle appeared.

This was Trinity. A cybersex site.

Cybersex: a "modern service," as the site put it, allowing users to have sex-like experiences via the internet rather than in the flesh. Usually, sites like this add all sorts of things—photos, video, voice-enabled communication, avatars for navigating the virtual space—to the chat experience, blending cybersex with a dating or hookup site. But Trinity's special quality was its avoidance of these things. There was nothing besides the chat—no visuals, no audio—making for an experience both retro and novel.

Its slogan began with a quote from *The Little Prince.*

The most beautiful things in the world can't be seen or touched. Have authentic encounters and find your true soul mate—here.

I opened my inbox and found a message waiting for me. It was from Cerberus.

My heart fluttered as my excitement rose. I tapped the message to open it.

As the slogan promises, all that's in the chat is text—not even any icons next to the names.

>> I'm watchng the torch relay

>> I'd rather have you grip *my* torch instead

>> It's getting quite hard already

Cerberus is the name of the three-headed hound of the underworld in Greek mythology. The name apparently means *the phantom from the bottomless pit.* Rather spooky for a chat handle, but I've always liked dogs more than cats anyway, and besides, Cerberus was the only person I'd been able to have a sustained chat with since joining the site.

I thought for a moment, then replied to him.

<< Your torch is always welcome

<< You caught me with my panties already down

That's true enough, I thought, sitting there on the toilet with my underwear at my ankles. I continued typing.

<< Push it in all the way

I hit send.

When I did, my phone made a sound—*shooom!*—as if something were flying off somewhere.

I saw the dots appear that meant Cerberus was typing a response.

>> I wanted to be the one to pull your panties down

>> But now I'm touching myself, imagining taking you from behind, thrusting hard

I was getting excited, and I answered immediately.

<< I'm touching myself too. My finger is inside

<< Ohhhh

<< I think I might start moaning if I'm not careful . . .

I'm not even sure if this sort of thing is what people mean when they say *cybersex*. But after all, regular sex takes many forms depending on who's doing it, so why wouldn't sex via text be the same? Whatever the case, we'd been chatting like this for two weeks now—definitely a record. I could feel a small hope forming in my heart that I may have found my *true soul mate*.

>> I'm so hard

>> I can't last much longer

<< I’m so wet

<< I won’t last much longer either . . .

It seemed like it was time to meet in person. But I couldn’t bring myself to be the one to propose it.

With other guys I’d been chatting with, they’d been the ones intent on meeting as soon as possible, but when it came time to actually do it, they’d suddenly send a rude message like *How could I get it up for an old lady like you?* and break off contact. Maybe it was partly my fault for stupidly telling them my real age. Though it was a shock to get such messages. I’d certainly never considered myself an “old lady”—an elderly woman!—before.

>> Ahhh!

>> Ohhh. Mmmmm . . .

I called out with my body in this heat.

<< Ahhhhh . . .

<< Ahhhhhh! Ahhhhhhh!

I called out with my body, to Cerberus.
I didn’t care what he might look like.
He could be fat or bald or even old—it didn’t matter at all.

<< It’s so good

<< So good . . . ahhhhh

<< Ahhhhh

Cerberus and I sent a variety of moans back and forth to each other. Finally, we exchanged a series of *I'm coming! I'm coming! I'm coming, too!* messages as well.

My phone still in hand, I used toilet paper to carefully wipe away the blood that had flowed from between my legs and stood up. The water in the toilet was dyed pale red.

Looking down at it, I saw myself in the blood-drenched eggs my ovaries had created just to shed, saw my day-to-day life, my existence itself, as so much empty waste, flowing forth to be flushed away, to disappear completely, meaninglessly, creating nothing, being nothing.

I resisted this feeling with all my might.

I wanted to be supported.

I wanted to be saved.

Looking down at my stomach, I traced the crooked lines of my stretch marks with my fingers.

After all, I wasn't alone.

Would my daughter save me? Well, even if she didn't, she might have a daughter, and that daughter might have a daughter, and that daughter might have a daughter, too. I imagined the single thread connecting me to my daughter and her daughter and to all the daughters to come, a thread connecting the past to the future that bound us together and gave me the strength to turn and unroll a bit more paper from the roll. I used it to diligently scrub the blood from the inside of my underwear.

Regretting my decision that morning to put on khaki-colored pants, I untucked my white rayon blouse so it could flow down over my waist.

I looked to my right and saw the Olympic mascot scrawled on the bathroom wall.

I left the restroom and headed straight for the convenience store in the station. I went to the aisle farthest from and opposite the magazine display at the front, pulling both pads and tampons off the shelf and walking quickly to the counter.

The middle-aged man in front of me waiting to pay for his tuna-filled rice ball and his plastic bottle of "special reserve" green tea glanced back at me, then averted his eyes in seeming disgust. The dark-skinned boy behind the counter, who might have been an exchange student, carefully wrapped the tampons and pads in a brown paper sack before placing them in a plastic bag to hand back to me.

I got out my card to pay.

An electronic bell sounded, and money passed invisibly between us.

¥547

All that was visible of the transaction was the price on the LCD screen as it appeared, then disappeared.

IT WAS RUSH hour on the Saikyō Line, but the train was unusually empty. Or rather, there were people standing here and there, making it seem crowded, but when I entered, the seats to the left opposite the door were all unfilled. I noticed a kempt old man sitting alone, right in the middle of all those empty seats. He was wearing a white Ralph Lauren polo shirt and a smart hunting cap. He looked to be about seventy years old, and by all appearances seemed like any other retiree on his way to enjoy a round of golf.

A young man in a business suit rushed in, wiping his forehead with his handkerchief, and went to sit down beside the old man, then gave a little yelp and jumped immediately back up when he caught a closer look at him.

I looked at the old man's right hand.

Of course.

His hand was gripping a shiny black stone.

An "accursed stone"!

I shrank back away from him, but the door slid shut behind me, and the train slowly began to move.

The air-conditioning was so strong it was almost cold. And there was nowhere to run.

My heart raced as I looked right, then left. The old man continued to sit where he was, unmoving, staring into space. Everyone else on the train car had turned to stare at him. I could feel the tension rising in the cramped space.

The train took a curve. I could see streets lined with houses passing by outside the windows. The train lines had been extended out farther and farther, connecting suburban neighborhoods like mine to the center as they continued their spread. Such a peaceful summer scene out there.

As I watched, the old man slowly brought his left hand to the breast pocket of his shirt. A high school girl standing behind me exclaimed under her breath, *"Oh shit!"*

What was he going to take out of that pocket?

It was very possible he meant to release radioactive material into the train car.

I took a deep breath and braced myself.

A man standing next to me had his phone out, his finger on the red record button. Perhaps he was broadcasting live, or perhaps he wanted to have evidence of what was about to happen for later.

I tried to remember what I was supposed to do in the event of exposure to radioactive material. Use a handkerchief to cover my mouth and nose? Rinse any affected area with water? Was that it? But in a small space like this, if the material was intensely radioactive, we were all exposed already.

The old man had withdrawn whatever it was from his pocket. It was an object covered in gold foil.

I could hear rustling all around me, everyone murmuring in alarm. People drew back even farther from the old man, forming a large semicircle around him. A woman carrying her baby in a Baby Björn let out a small scream and dove for the back of the crowd, bumping me and making me cry out involuntarily as well.

The old man, still holding the shiny black rock in one hand, began fiddling with the foil-wrapped object.

I couldn't stop staring at him.

Cold sweat ran down my sides.

I wanted to leap straight off the moving train.

I regretted not bringing my Geiger counter with me.

Finally, the old man managed to peel off the gold foil. A lump of some sort of thick, muddy-looking substance was revealed.

Everyone held their breath.

The old man, without a moment's hesitation, brought the object to his mouth. And then took a bite!

The rest of the object quickly followed the first bite down the old man's throat.

He ate it! He ate the radioactive material!

I watched his every move, shivering with fear.

But then—I smelled a faint, sweet smell. Looking closer, I realized that the foil-wrapped object had merely been a melty chocolate bar. The train car fell silent, and the only sound that remained was that of the old man chewing his chocolate.

Seriously?

The man filming the proceedings next to me with his phone let out a defeated sigh. Here and there in the crowd, I even heard giggles.

Relieved as well, I looked behind me at the train car door. On the monitor mounted above it, white numbers flashed against a red background, counting down:

10

9

8

7

6

5

4

3

2

1 . . .

At Last!

The Tokyo Olympics Have Arrived!

Opening Ceremony Today!

This was followed by an animation of a large *kusudama* cracker breaking open. Flags from every country spilled out, accompanied by doves. And then the Olympic Rings appeared, in front of a checkered pattern of light blue and white.

The train slid into the next station. As soon as the door opened, I swam against the stream of boarding bodies so I could run onto a neighboring car.

IT WAS ABOUT nine years ago that we began spotting old people carrying "accursed stones" around in our neighborhood.

It had been a dark spring. It was the year of the great earthquake and tsunami and the nuclear accident in Fukushima, and we experienced planned blackouts here, too, making the season literally dark as well.

My daughter was three then, and I'd just moved back in with my mother, so I had no money to leave for the relative safety of the west. Besides, the idea of packing everything up and fleeing somewhere was absolutely out of the question for my mother. My sister, too, found herself with a pause in her work, so she moved back home, the three of us suddenly living together again in this quiet suburban town.

It was chilly that day, with cloudy skies since morning and light rain just beginning to fall.

I looked out the window and saw my mother walking out into the garden without even an umbrella.

My daughter was out there too, playing under the fig tree with a bag of animal crackers clutched in her hand.

I started running immediately, yelling after them.

What did she think she was doing?

Taking her out without telling me, in the middle of this rain? And letting her eat all the sweets she wants?

Drenched, my daughter was gleefully shoveling animal crackers into her mouth.

Doesn't she know it's not just water—it's radioactivity falling too?

I rushed out the front door, irritated, and was heading toward the garden when it happened. I looked up and saw an old man alone, staggering down the hill toward the house.

It was Sasaki's grandfather. He'd been a great man in his day, the CEO of a big construction company or some such, and more recently he'd been serving as the chair of the local city council. But now he was lurching along with his white-flecked hair sticking out every which way, wearing a tank top with no shirt over it. He held a black stone in one hand that glittered as he made his way down the road, one leg dragging behind him.

I'd heard a rumor that two weeks after the earthquake, he'd gone to the bathroom in the middle of the night and collapsed from a small stroke, and he'd been not quite there ever since. Though it seemed now that that might have been an understatement.

The old man's bird's nest of hair was getting soaked in the rain, sticking to his forehead and cheeks. His eyes shone with vacant fervor.

I stood rooted to the spot, watching him. He seemed not to notice me at all, his gaze never diverting from a fixed stare.

His hand was gripping the black stone too hard, and I could see even from afar that his fingers were turning white from the strain.

Sasaki's grandfather suddenly halted his progress down the hill. He brought the stone in his hand to his ear with some force, almost hitting himself with it.

There was blood oozing from the area around his ear. He quietly closed his eyes. The blood mixed with the rain and slid slowly down his cheek to form drops that fell to the ground.

My mother and daughter joined me where I stood, all of us transfixed by the sight of him.

A vending machine across the street, its LCD screen turned off due to energy conservation measures, stood facing the scene, shiny and dark as a monolith.

"Can you hear it?"

A low voice spoke right behind me, startling me. It was my sister, who had emerged from the house at some point. Rainwater ran down her cheeks.

DURING THIS TIME, elderly people suffering from dementia began, one by one, to walk around holding "accursed stones" in their hands. Or at least that's what people started calling them. What the old people were holding were just rocks they'd picked up somewhere, but they were always shiny and black, and this eerie consistency led to the term "accursed stones." It wasn't clear exactly where the name itself came from.

It might have simply been that seeing a stone in an old person's hand seemed to portend that something bad was about to happen. But it could also have come from *pitchblende*, the German term for uraninite—*pitch* for "dark" or "accursed," *blende* for "ore." And it was true that when these "accursed stones" came in contact with a Geiger counter, the radiation readings would go up—though others pointed out that stones like granite and marble often contain tiny veins of radioactive ore as a matter of course, so there was no obvious link to be made.

What did seem clear was that once old people held these stones in their hands, they began acting as if possessed.

Or, to be more precise, they began to act as if *possessed by radiation.*

The old people would put the accursed stones to their ears, listening intently as if to a voice coming from within them. And then they would start talking nonstop about radiation.

What they said was sometimes shockingly astute, as if, in place of the memories they'd lost, they'd gained the memories of radiation itself (if such a thing could be said to exist). Old men and women who'd never even graduated from primary school were suddenly spouting all sorts of knowledge, from simple $E=mc^2$-style equations to deriving the Schwarzschild solution on their own—accounts like this began to circulate widely, and it was hard to tell truth from fiction.

On top of this, old people carrying stones would gravitate toward radioactive materials, as if drawn to them by a beckoning voice. People made jokes about it: if you're trying to detect hot spots, instead of using a Geiger counter, just look for a bunch of old people gathered in one place.

They were like moths drawn to a flame.

As long as there was fire, they were powerless not to fly into it.

But even worse, they didn't just fly into fire, they tried to bring it back with them.

They tried to carry fire in their own hands.

The Prometheus trick.

The old people seemed compelled, once they discovered radioactive material, to gather up as much as they could and put it all in one place.

It was becoming quite an issue.

I was in Setagaya, performing maintenance on a water purifier we'd installed in the home of a woman named Sawada, when she began talking to me about it, absently stroking the white hair she'd permed and dyed light purple.

"It's like I'm living in Palestine here. All the old people are walking around carrying rocks in their hands."

Sawada-san explained that she'd seen on the news that in Palestine, everyone, young and old alike, carried stones to throw at tanks and military vehicles. I listened to her talk as I lay on her kitchen floor, fiddling with a bolt on the purifier with my hexagonal wrench.

Sawada-san peered down at me as I worked, and then asked, her eyes wide, "Does that purifier remove everything? Including, you know—radiation?"

People said it was the radiation released by the nuclear accident that caused the old people to pick up the accursed stones. There were rumors that after Chernobyl, in places even as far away as Kyiv, the same phenomenon had happened. There were even urban legends telling of old people picking up accursed stones in the wake of the bombings of Hiroshima and Nagasaki. In places with known veins of uranium ore, not only old people, but the young, too, begin to carry stones, they said.

There were so many rumors, it was hard to separate what might be true from what might be false.

It was evident how easily people could be manipulated by news that seemed obviously fake.

And yet, this was a time when the real news showed footage of a nuclear reactor exploding in a cloud of white gas beneath the clear blue sky, or offered accounts of workers using shredded newspaper to plug the flood of contaminated water from a structure created as the highest expression of scientific knowledge. It was a time when reality itself seemed obviously fake.

Summer followed spring, and the cicadas hardly made a sound.

The radiation killed them, people said.

That's what people said, and the rumor spread far and wide, but on the television, they attributed it to normal variations in temperature—some years it's too cold or too hot and they die in their eggs before hatching.

In the supermarkets, packages of mushrooms were displayed with stickers saying they'd been tested for radioactivity; mothers with Geiger counters walked along the routes their children took to school, monitoring the radiation levels.

My daughter, as she played inside, would put a bright-colored plastic toy to her ear, imitating the old man she'd seen.

But I reminded myself that there were trendy obsessions with the paranormal back when I was growing up, too—spoon-bending, table-turning séances, sending messages to UFOs.

My daughter whispered in my ear.

Can you hear it?

9:30

I slid my card through the electronic reader. A chime sounded as money invisibly drained from my account.

Remaining Balance: ¥3,420

The fare was paid; unseen forces unlocked the gate to let me through.

I walked through the turnstile and left the station building, and the wet heat hit me again. I pulled my gloves back up to my elbows, slid my sunglasses back on, and opened my silver umbrella once more over my head. I bore my aching abdomen as best as I could as I headed toward the office.

I passed through the rows of bus stops and began to cut across the plaza on the other side. The plaza was paved in stone and decorated with several large flower-beds filled with red salvia. Only a few years ago, it had been covered in the blue tarps and cardboard of homeless encampments, but now they were nowhere to be found. Naturally, the stray plastic bottles and empty liquor bottles had also disappeared, along with the cheap broken umbrellas. Surely the cleanup here had been thanks, as so much was, to the Olympics. Approaching the center of the plaza, I noticed that the corners of some of the planters were broken, with bricks missing and clumps of soil and salvia plants strewn, roots and all, across the paving stones. Either due to their roots being exposed or simply having reached the end of their life cycle, the salvia blossoms, once a vivid red, had begun to darken and wither.

The sight of them immediately brought to mind the old man I'd seen on the train car earlier, making my chest hurt.

That muddy brown mass covered in foil.

The black stone gripped in his other hand, the way it glittered in places.

I was hurrying to reach the boulevard on the other side of the stone-paved plaza when it happened—I tripped and pitched forward, my body rushing toward the ground. My silver umbrella flew into the air. My head collided with the stones as one of my pumps fell off my foot and rolled across the ground.

Moaning, I raised my head and looked around, glaring.

The stray rocks strewn randomly across the plaza suddenly reminded me of the accursed stones, and I shivered.

I crawled around the area, reaching out with my hands to gather first my stray pump, then my umbrella, from where they'd fallen. As I did, my eyes lit upon a small rock lying there, so innocently, on the paving stones. I couldn't tell if it was a paving stone that had loosened from its setting, or if it was just a rock fallen from somewhere else, or if someone had deliberately set it there.

Whatever the case, I resolved to take the godforsaken thing with me and throw it in the garbage. I picked it up and stuffed it in my bag.

If the Olympics really wanted to be useful, I muttered to myself, they wouldn't just clear away the homeless people, they'd clear away these loose stones, too—they'd clear away every rock in the city, in the country!

Just like I'd had to clear everything out of that house.

IT WAS LAST autumn when we began talking about selling the house—our mother's house.

Our mother had reached for a fig from the tree in the garden and fallen, breaking her leg.

Once she stopped being able to walk, it didn't take long for our mother to start forgetting things. Barely a month had passed and she'd lost her house keys three times; soon she lost the ability to complete a piece of lace, spending her time looping yarn over and over with no seeming purpose or end.

Nevertheless, we persisted in taking her to rehab. We used funds from the city to install, against Mother's half-crazed protests, shiny plastic railings in the bathroom and along the wall in the stairwell.

My sister proclaimed, "You know, we'll make more on it if we sell before the Olympics."

She added, "If we move her into a new apartment, we can make it so there's no steps for her, easy."

In other words, if we were to sell the land the house sat on to a developer in anticipation of the Olympics, we could afford to put Mother in a new high-rise apartment somewhere.

"A nurse takes money, though. She needs someone there to help her."

My sister proposed a solution.

"Paying rent to live on our own just seems like a waste at this point—I think we should all move in together. An apartment set up would work for that. If we put the money down and take out a loan, we could do it."

It was, honestly, an appealing prospect.

After moving back to this house with my daughter after the divorce, I really had nowhere to go.

So, my sister and I began to work, secretly, on selling the house.

Our mother was still alive, but in truth, she was beginning to forget even this house she'd cared so deeply about for so long. Though it was a bit ironic that this place, constructed fifty-six years ago in the run-up to one Olympics, was going to be torn down now in anticipation of another one.

. . .

WE BEGAN TO clean and pack up the house around the same time as the start of the Olympic torch relay. On March 26, a Thursday, the sacred fire was brandished with much fanfare at the J-Village National Soccer Training Center in Fukushima. The center had served as the base of operations during the 2011 Fukushima Dai-ichi nuclear disaster. We spent that day folding cardboard to make boxes. My sister had already gotten rid of her place to avoid the waste of continuing to pay rent, and she and her modest pile of possessions were moving in at the end of the month.

It was now Saturday, and the television showed the torch passing through some sort of mountainous area. We'd delivered Mother to the day service, and now my daughter and I were cleaning up the first floor while my sister attended to the second. Loud music blared from the speakers in the living room, thanks to my daughter's favorite band: DEATH BE NOT PROUD.

You are slave to Fate
To Chance, to Kings
To Desperate Men.
You dwell with Poison,
War, and Sickness.
With charms and poppies
we fall asleep
like we do with you,
maybe better
than we do with you . . .

A female vocalist was intoning these lyrics over a looped beat. My daughter, outfitted in a black shirt, black jeans, and a black face mask for the dust, was bobbing her head along with the music as she walked back and forth between the living room and the room where my mother's bed had been placed.

I was cleaning out the stained-glass china cabinet in the corner of the living room.

I was taking each plate out one by one. The flower pattern and gold edging had rubbed off a bit, but I couldn't tell if this was due to them being antiques or just old and worn out. I decided it didn't matter to me, and I stacked them in the translucent garbage bag on the floor beside me without really looking at them.

One short sleep and we
awaken for eternity,
And at that moment,
Death, you shall be no more!
Death, you will be the one to die!

My sister came down from the second floor and walked into the living room, her face mask pulled down around her chin.

"What is this noise?"

My daughter launched into an earnest explanation of how the band based their lyrics on Elizabethan poet John Donne's Holy Sonnets and how this particular song was based on the sonnet where they also got their name, but my sister just ignored her and headed straight for the garbage bag of plates at my feet.

"If we put this on eBay, I bet we could get a good price . . ." My sister was pulling a gold-rimmed plate back out of the bag when it happened.

The room went silent.

My sister and I both turned to look at my daughter. She was standing, staring at the television, the remote control in her hand. She pressed a button and an unseen force raised the volume.

The news was on.

We could hear the voice of a female newscaster.

The torch relay was no longer being shown.

"What is this . . . ?"

The words escaped my sister's mouth as she stood transfixed, the plate in her hand now forgotten.

The television was showing an old man throwing a huge stack of ¥10,000 bills in the air.

The clear blue sky was filled with fluffy white clouds that were joined now with fluttering bills, with money.

"There must be a hundred million there . . . " my sister murmured, wonderingly.

The man dressed in his khaki jacket looked to be around eighty. He had a duffel bag slung over his shoulder that looked too big for his body, and he was reaching into it, taking out handfuls of money, and throwing them in the air.

Occasionally, the camera would show a pyramid-shaped structure in the background—was it the National Diet Building? There was a group of middle-aged women wearing face masks who might have been there to see the cherry blossoms along the Chidori-ga-fuchi Moat, as well as a group of uniformed junior high school students whose presence was a total mystery, and they were all now crowding around the man as if taking part in a festival. They were grabbing at the bills fluttering the air, trying to gather as many as they could. Students with the pockets of their uniforms stuffed with money turned to flash peace signs at the camera.

My sister finally returned the plate in her hand to the stack in the bag.

"We've got to go get some, right?"

She took out her phone and began to look for the best route to get there.

"We might get there on time if we leave right now! The wind is strong, there could be tons of bills blown all over the place that we could find if we look. They say if you find money and no one claims it after a month, it's yours, but I wonder if that would apply in a situation like this . . ."

My sister was talking to herself in an excited monologue. She continued, "Where did that old guy get that money in the first place anyway? Well, maybe it was his savings, old people have savings . . . or the lottery? Or is it drug money? It looks kind of like money you might get that way. Or it's money laundering? It's like a real-life *Breaking Bad*! Or an old fairy tale, like you cut open a stalk of bamboo and there's a billion yen, or two billion . . . Anyway, look at those ladies, they're doing pretty well for themselves, aren't they? And look at that kid, he must have ¥100,000 in his pocket! We need to go, you guys, we need to get some of that!"

In the end, though, it looked like it would take over an hour to get to the Diet Building no matter which route we picked, so we reached the conclusion that there would surely not be a single

¥10,000 bill left once we arrived. After finally giving up, my sister went back to cleaning up the second floor, and I eventually went up to join her.

As we opened the door to our father's study, I remembered his magic trick blowing on the envelope of money. I also thought of the old folk tale he'd tell us about the old man who made dead trees bloom—the old man at the Diet Building reminded me of him, too.

It had been close to thirty years since our father had passed away, but his study was still largely the same. There was still the shelf with its display of geological specimens all lined up. Dust danced lazily in the sunlight filtering through the lace curtains hanging in the windows.

Once upon a time, there was an old man, an old woman, and a dog named Pooch.

One day, Pooch went out into the garden and said, "Arf arf! Dig here!"

Our father would tell us the story in his study.

The old man followed Pooch's instructions and started to dig.

Soon, he found a gold coin!

But the old man's neighbor grew jealous of his fortune, and he killed Pooch.

The old man cried and cried and buried poor Pooch in the garden.

Before long, a tree began to grow from where Pooch was buried.

And when the old man cut into the tree, gold coins flowed forth.

But the old man's neighbor was even more jealous now, and he lit the tree on fire, burning it to the ground.

The old man cried and cried, and gathered the tree's ashes, and then scattered them around the garden.

And once he did, old cherry trees that had withered and died began to bloom again.

Soon, a rich daimyo came to see the marvel.

"Let us see you make a dead tree bloom," he commanded.

The daimyo was very impressed with what he saw, and he gave the old man piles and piles of gold coins.

As he wound up the story, our father would add his own ending.

If we dig into the ground, we'll find treasure too!

And then he would proudly point to his row of specimens.

Do you think I'm lying? Let's dig into the ground ourselves and find out!

My sister and I would start giggling as he would mime digging into the carpet that lay atop the study's oak floor.

All right, what did we find?

My sister and I would keep our eyes on his fingertips as we shook our heads.

Our father would then make grabbing motions with his fingers.

And he would blow into the air.

And then, slowly, he would open his hand for us to see.

There it would be, a glittering piece of mica or pyrite. Fool's gold.

Sometimes it would be a semiprecious stone, like quartz or amethyst.

Our father loved rocks as much as he loved magic. He loved rocks so much that he even, through an acquaintance, got a job at a company that made gravestones.

It was true what he said, that when you dig in the ground, you find treasure—after all, it was through the gravestone job that he met our mother. She'd visited the company he worked for looking to use the inheritance from her rich family to buy a memorial tablet for her parents.

My sister and I, clad in masks and work gloves, walked into the study.

We opened up the doors of the built-in cabinet under the bookshelves, pulling out boxes of rocks and mineral specimens that we ended up putting straight in the garbage bag. As we didn't know exactly what category of trash a bunch of rocks belonged in—noncombustible?—we were at a bit of loss as to what to do. There were a few glasses and vases made of fluorescent green glass, too. We put those in the garbage bag as well.

My sister found a wristwatch in his desk drawer.

Our mother had given it to him for his birthday.

She'd found it in an antique shop owned by an old friend from junior high.

It was marked *Westclox USA 1920,* and the numbers on its dial glowed fluorescent green.

My sister grabbed it with her work glove and shoved it in the garbage bag.

I cinched the bag's mouth shut tight and carried it out to the garden to set beneath the fig tree.

EVENING CAME, AND my sister took the trouble to walk all the way to the pizza place near the station to get dinner. It was a delivery place, but you got a free pie if you picked up your order yourself.

Our mother had returned from the day service and was sitting on the deep-green velvet sofa like always, her golden needles in her hands, concentrating on trying to crochet some lace as if she didn't even notice all the changes that had occurred in the room while she'd been away. She looped and looped the yarn without ever completing a stitch, the same bit running back and forth through her fingers until it turned a grimy black.

My daughter was sitting cross-legged in the midst of the dishes that had yet to be packed, her eyes glued to the television. The female newscaster was on again.

At approximately one o'clock this afternoon, the suspect, Ken'ichi Tani, age eighty two, began to distribute ¥10,000 bills in front of the National Diet Building—

A photograph of the old man appeared in a box to the newscaster's upper right side. The image was grainy, as if the original photo had been over-enlarged.

Radioactive material had been discovered on the bills. Footage ran showing a ¥10,000 bill against a black background, illuminated by a spotlight. A gloved hand holding a Geiger counter appeared, and it began to go off as it was held near the money. The dial read 70–130 mSv/h.

We were all glued to the television at this point. Except Mother, who'd fallen asleep on her perch on the green sofa, her golden needles still in her hands.

The newscaster continued, a grave look on her face.

There is no reason to believe there will be any adverse effect on public health. Nonetheless, if you find any bills you suspect may have been contaminated, in order to prevent the further spread of contamination, please do not use them and instead bring them to the nearest police station right away.

The email address and telephone number to contact appeared on-screen.

The suspect appears to have lived alone in a single-family dwelling in the Suginami District of Tokyo. The suspect also stated he was from an area now called Jáchymov in the Czech Republic, which used to be called Sankt Joachimsthal, in former Bohemia. Authorities are investigating any possible links to terrorist organizations at this time.

Sankt Joachimsthal. Saint Joachim's Valley.

My breath stopped in my throat as I heard the name.

My sister walked in right at that moment, brandishing pizza boxes as she entered the living room.

"Turned out to be an even better idea than I thought to go pick these up—there was a little drawing where you pick a prize at the cash register, and I got two free Cokes! How lucky can you get, right?"

My sister pulled the Cokes out of her pockets one by one to show us, her scarf still wrapped around her neck. It was only after the pizzas were set out on the Art Deco dining table and divided onto paper plates that my sister took notice of what was happening on the television.

"Oh man—on the money? Shit!"

Cheese and tomato sauce spilled off the edge of the paper plates onto the white lace tablecloth.

My daughter helped our mother into her seat at the table, then sat cross-legged in her own seat, her eyes on the phone in her hand.

Saint Joachimsthal, in former Bohemia, present-day Jáchymov in the Czech Republic.

Saint Joachim's Valley.

My heart raced.

My daughter unhooked a keychain hanging from her belt and held it out to me in her palm.

"I just found this cleaning up."

The keychain had a coin attached to it, about the size of a ¥500 piece.

One side had a picture of a lion standing on its hind legs, while the other showed a bearded man and letters spelling JOACHIM.

Naturally, that was Saint Joachim.

I hadn't forgotten that keychain, or the *thaler* decorating it. Nor the postcard my mother had sent showing the photo of a grand hotel nestled in a valley surrounded by mountains. Saint Joachimsthal, Saint Joachim's Valley. I remember clearly even now what she'd written so neatly with her fountain pen on the other side.

Mitsuko and I are in a town called Jáchymov, three hours away from Prague by bus. This is the hotel where we're staying—it looks like a castle. People call it the Radium Palace!

There's a museum in town, they have a lot of rare minerals on display. Imagine how much your father would have liked that! Tomorrow we're going to a hot spring town Goethe loved, called Carlsbad.

I expect your little one is already starting to kick! I can't believe I'm about to be a grandmother.

I hope you're looking forward to seeing what I got you!

Talk to you again soon.

My sister answered my daughter before I had a chance to.

"Oh yeah, that coin. Mother gave both of us one as a souvenir."

She took a bite of her chicken-teriyaki-and-avocado pizza as she spoke.

"From when she went to the Czech Republic, right? With her tacky friend, the one who got nabbed for tax evasion—you remember, she had that antique store."

"Mitsuko . . ." I said, staring up at the ceiling.

That's where Mother bought that watch for our father, too—at Mitsuko's store.

And Mitsuko *was* tacky, wearing so much perfume that I could always tell when Mother spent time with her from the smell. But she and our mother got along somehow. After our father died, Mother began to work part-time at Mitsuko's shop, even giving lacemaking classes at one point.

My sister was still talking, loading up her plate with another slice.

"Yeah, Mitsuko, that's it. Remember when the taxi ripped them off on the way to that place, Saint Something-something? She really blew up. Mother said she was so angry, it was epic. It's funny thinking about it now, her being a tax cheat and all."

It had been Mitsuko who'd invited Mother on that trip.

You'll cheer up when your grandchild arrives, but you'll also be busier, have less time to go on trips and do things for yourself!

Mitsuko had said this to Mother while pointing at my swelling belly.

That trip was supposed to have been for antique hunting. So how did they end up all the way in Jáchymov? Well, Mitsuko did seem like one to go for spas and hot spring resorts. And maybe Mom was interested in the Goethe connection. It was three hours from Prague—the right distance for a quick jaunt to stretch their legs and relax.

It wasn't such a strange coincidence that Mother happened to have stopped by there once, I told myself.

And yet. Still.

When I received that postcard from Mother. Or when she handed me that keychain when she got back.

I'd had the thought.

That I should get rid of it, just throw it away.

I couldn't tell whether or not my daughter was listening to us talk; she seemed absorbed in looking at the coin resting in her hand as she closed her fingers over it, then opened them again. *Why can't it be like a magic trick, and the coin would disappear for good?* But, of course, even a trick wasn't really magic—the coin would remain no matter how many times she hid it with her hand.

Mother, despite being the topic of conversation, continued chewing on her corn-and-potato pizza without a word as if she couldn't hear us.

The television was airing footage of the old man with the bag of money being grabbed from both sides by policemen and dragged away.

I used my finger to scrape at the cheese so I could pick out the toppings to eat one by one.

The newscaster continued her report.

It's unclear at this time what motivated the attack, or how the suspect was able to contaminate the bills with radioactive material.

On-screen, footage showed money spilling out of the old man's duffel bag as he was marched away. The crowd of middle-aged women followed close behind, stuffing the bills in their pockets.

Then, just as he was being pressed into the back of the police car, we could clearly see something drop from his hand onto the ground.

A black stone, shiny in places.

Accursed.

The newscaster continued, oblivious.

The suspect had past experience working at a nuclear research facility, and investigators are now looking into any possible mismanagement of radioactive materials at that facility.

She went on to say that the suspect had been diagnosed as suffering from dementia two years previously.

A shiver ran through my body as I listened. And then it happened.

I heard a strange sound just behind my head.

Gragragragra, gorogorogorogorogoro . . .

Looking behind me, I saw that it was Mother. She'd poured Coke in her mouth and was gargling it.

Gragragra, gorogorogorogoro

Gragragragra, gorgoro, gorogorgorgorgorororororo . . .

The gargling was loud enough to drown out the television.

Thankfully, instead of spitting it out, she swallowed it.

The screen was filled with ¥10,000 bills, old ones. Over and over, the face of Prince Shotoku, the *Heavenly-being-from-whence-the-sun-rises.*

. . .

THAT NIGHT I tossed and turned in bed and didn't sleep a wink. I stared at the rose-patterned wallpaper, picking out where it was stained even in the dark. Ever since she hurt her leg, Mother had been sleeping on the first floor in what had been my room, since that's where we'd put the moveable electric hospital bed we rented. That meant that now I slept in her room, in her bed. This simple switch seemed to complete our recent exchange of roles, and I couldn't get comfortable in my new surroundings.

I could see all too clearly through the half-open door the shiny plastic railing we'd installed in the hallway. In the corner of the room, I saw where my mother's treasures—the vanity with the gold-framed mirror, the embroidered ottoman, and all the rest—were stacked up. Most of that stuff was going to be left behind in the move; I supposed it would just be disposed of along with the house itself, in the end.

The old man who'd been distributing the money was apparently under the delusion he'd been buried in the ground at the bottom of Saint Joachim's Valley. They said he couldn't stop talking about it.

I was in a deep dark hole beneath the soil, he reportedly said.

But one day, someone dug me out, and I was brought into the light.

Men came and dug me out.

They spoke German and came from Saxony, questing for silver.

They used the silver they mined to make coins that soon spread all over Bohemia.

The coins were called thalers, *from* Sankt Joachimsthal, *the name of this land.*

Eventually the thalers *even made their way to the New World, where they came to be called* dollars*—for this is the origin of the dollar.*

So yes, I was dug out of the ground with the silver, then discarded.

I was merely a shiny black stone, after all.

Soon I was the only stone that emerged anymore, no silver, just me: shiny, black, worthless.

Not only that, but the men began to suffer a mysterious malady.

Their lungs would weaken, their bodies would drag, they would bleed without stopping.

Was it this worthless stone, they wondered?

Was it me?

They began to despise me, call me pitchblende.

Accursed stone.

Accursed.

I jumped out of bed and went to the window, and then, trepidatiously, pressed my forehead to the glass and looked down.

There it was, in the dark garden next to the fig tree: the translucent garbage bag filled with the things from Father's study. The vases, the wristwatch, the geological specimens—they were all still in the bag, its mouth cinched tight. Noncombustible garbage pickup was only once a week. I didn't relish the prospect of seeing that bag out there for six more days.

By the time I woke up the next day, an article on the internet talking about the amount of money that had been distributed by the old man had already caused quite a stir.

The amount was ¥235,000,000.

The article pointed out that this was the same amount of money the Japanese Parliament approved to begin developing nuclear power capability again after the war. A number reportedly chosen because it corresponded to that of the isotope uranium-235.

The same March that this budget was approved, the tuna and fishermen aboard the *Lucky Dragon Number 5* were blasted by nuclear radiation near Bikini Atoll. The United States had conducted a test of its hydrogen bomb, Bravo, and rained radiation down on the area. The tuna onboard, now fearfully called atomic tuna, ended up buried in the ground beneath the Tsukiji Fish Market.

Years later, when construction was taking place to excavate the Ōedo subway line and, later, to displace Tsukiji to make room for the Olympics, the whole area was dug up, but no trace of atomic tuna was ever found—not even bones. Theorists on the internet said this new radioactive incident was the curse of the atomic tuna.

I lay on my bed, phone in hand, and scrolled through the article.

Nine years after the ¥235-million budget was allocated to develop nuclear power and the atomic tuna was buried beneath Tsukiji, the first light bulb powered by Japanese nuclear energy switched on in a town called Tōkai, in Ibaraki Prefecture.

And the following year, the Olympics arrived in Tokyo.

Looking around my mother's dimly lit bedroom, I found it unsettling to think that this house had been built at the same time as the Olympics. An old photo of my mother and father, just married and a year away from constructing this house, hung in an antique gold frame on the rose-patterned wall. Mother in her white mini dress, Father in his tight pants: both looked into the camera, smiling. The ground they were standing on was the ground this house was built on.

There was nothing there then. Not even the fig tree.

It was making me ill to look at, so I took the photo off the wall.

There was a large black stain behind it, like a dark fortune.

THREE DAYS LATER, there was an announcement from the government.

They stated that it was possible that the suspect did not suffer from dementia, but rather from a previously unknown ailment with unclear causes.

While this disease may resemble dementia in its initial stages, as it advances, sufferers begin to pick up rocks and hold them to their ears. They become attracted to materials with high levels of radioactivity, and they are driven to try to collect them. They begin to suffer from aural hallucinations, and eventually descend into a state of delirium, prone to erratic speech and behavior.

The technical name for the disease was something long and in English.

But the initialism derived from it spelled TRINITY.

Trinity.

Now that it had a name, the condition could finally be talked about openly.

Trinity sufferers did not just try to gather radioactive materials and keep them in their rooms or in their pockets. They stuffed them in their mouths, or in any other orifices they could reach. And the first chance they got, they would take these materials and try to spread them as far and wide as possible.

Rumor had it that Trinities had actually existed for years.

An old woman who died some years ago was rumored to have been discovered with more than ten wristwatches with dials painted with radium paint inserted in her vagina.

During the same period, a body at a local crematorium was rumored to have yielded not just ashes and bones when it was burned but melted green glass. It turned out to be uranium glass.

More and more information began to circulate.

Trinities craved radioactivity like junkies crave their high, and they would go anywhere or do anything to get it. Several elderly Trinity sufferers were found trying to enter the exclusion zone surrounding the Fukushima Dai-ichi Nuclear Power Plant. There had been several incidents as well in which contaminated soil was removed from the containers where it had been temporarily stored, but the government had been keeping these quiet until now. Community groups also reported the theft of around a thousand bricks and paving stones from flowerbeds and roadside planters all over the country, bricks that could be traced to the roughly 1.5 million such building materials made from the gravel excavated during uranium-ore mining at Ningyō Pass.

Debates raged over these incidents, with some saying they were overblown by antinuclear activists, while others accused pro-nuclear, pro-government scientists of minimizing the situation for their own purposes.

It even became a staple horror setup for a while for someone, after the death of a dementia-suffering family member, to take a Geiger counter into the dead person's bedroom and find it to be radioactive.

Unease began to spread.

Carrying radioactive material like that is itself a terrorist act!

You could be exposed just by them passing you on the street or sitting next to you!

Trinities who saw that guy on television might be inspired to imitate him!

It's like in the U.S. after a mass shooting, there are likely to be copycats.

The scariest thing would be if someone, like that guy, who had specialized knowledge about nuclear radiation, suddenly turned Trinity.

They could hack into the nuclear energy system and cause a meltdown, or mix radioactive materials into the food or water supplies!

They're almost at the end of their lives anyway, they're like suicide bombers—they don't care if they get hurt!

THE OLD MAN who'd thrown the money had apparently written a post on Facebook shortly beforehand, which got tweeted and then retweeted tens of thousands of times:

I have suffered these past years from memory loss due to dementia. But now, the true memory loss afflicting me is not my own. It is that of all of you who fail to remember the past and remember the pain of that which cannot be seen.

If making visible the suffering and anguish of the invisible is terrorism, then call me a terrorist.

This is the beginning of the revenge of the invisible.

The beginning of the revenge of the invisible.

The elderly were now regarded as the most dangerous element of society.

Hospitals began to solicit people over sixty-five to come in and receive free Trinity tests. Some took issue with that, protesting that sixty-five was too young to be treated as an elderly potential terrorist, which in turn caused counterprotests insisting the opposite.

Advertisements showing happy, healthy seniors from all walks of life began airing on television, and posters showing winning poems from “Respect Our Elders” haiku contests were posted in the halls of elementary schools across Japan.

I—all of us, really—sat shivering, awaiting the cry of the Geiger counter.

10:00

All the way at the end of the dimly lit hallway on the fourth floor of the old multipurpose office building, I pushed open a frosted-glass door. I was greeted by stacks of water purification cartridges, and after winding my way through them, I found my four coworkers already at work readying packages for shipping.

Michiyo, the heavyset head of accounting, was checking the packing slips while fanning her ample, sweat-slicked bosom with an Olympics-sponsored checker-print hand-fan. The nails on her fingers as they gripped the fan stood out like barnacles.

"Everybody's so excited, Olympics this, Olympics that, but here we are, working our butts off on a national holiday in this dump. It's hard to feel much good cheer about that!"

Taki, the pallid sales manager, his spindly body bending in his ill-fitting suit under the weight of the cardboard boxes he was carrying back and forth, nodded his agreement. "You're so right!"

As she tore the packing slips off, Michiyo added, "Did you see the torch relay? It made me so mad!"

Tomi, the office manager, her hair bristling with pins, and Lee, with her unshaven arms, were putting the bonus gifts of hand towels into the boxes with the cartridges. They laughed in agreement.

"Oh yeah, everyone's talking about it!"

"Another pop idol's running today, I hear."

Michiyo snorted her contempt.

"I don't know what group she's from, EKG or BLT or whatever—the old coots who plan these things are so cynical. Makes me sick! They choose these cute girls or kids or people with disabilities—people where it's like, go ahead and run, who'd complain about someone like you? And it's almost like they're mocking them, you know, mocking the most powerless people in society by putting them out there like that."

Stacks of water purification cartridges designated for shipping were lined up on grey foam pads set out on the carpeted office floor. I reached into my bag and took out my thermos, filling my mouth with purified water. If only these purifiers could cleanse the hearts of these pitiful souls who couldn't even enjoy the Olympics! I looked out the window, but all that was visible through it was the dingy wall of the building next door.

. . .

THE NOT-SO-NEW APARTMENT into which we all moved after selling off the house was in an area of the suburbs that wasn't particularly convenient to get to from any train or subway station, but the one thing it had going for it was a great view.

Looking out the window, the sky spread out wide in all directions.

It was on the twenty-third floor. Some years back, someone living a few floors above had jumped to their death from their window—but to me, someone who'd never lived above the second floor in her life, the view was so refreshing and clean.

There were no steps in the place. The bath and toilet both had handrails already installed.

My mother's foot would have a chance to actually heal.

It seemed like a truly fresh start. Everything was on the way to getting better.

My daughter, buds plugged as always into her ears, leaned against the translucent resin railing on the balcony and told me about medieval Europe.

Apparently, people in those times believed that the higher you were, the healthier the air was, so the rich tried to live up as high as possible. They believed miasma—"bad air"—pooled in low places and caused disease. Elites lived as high as they could, ate birds that were as high-flying as they could, drank wine from grapes grown as high up in the mountains as they could. They were fearful of animals that crept along the ground and plants that grew close to the earth, and they endeavored to never let them pass their lips.

I walked out onto the balcony and leaned out over the railing to look down at the city.

"If only that were really true," I said.

The air was still chilly then, the sky a ceiling of white clouds.

SO BEGAN OUR new life.

When I happened to catch sight of them, the cardboard moving boxes stacked in the corners of the blindingly white rooms were the only reminders of the past, of the house we'd left behind.

As Golden Week approached, we decided to take care of them once and for all.

The first two days, my daughter and I got through about half the boxes ourselves. The third day, my daughter went off to Ikebukuro for a DEATH BE NOT PROUD concert she'd been saving up her allowance to attend, so my sister, who finally had a day off, and I sent Mother to the day service and applied ourselves to unpacking the rest.

Our progress was slow, though—nothing seemed to be actually coming out of the boxes.

The problem was that all we had left were things we'd stuffed into boxes just to be done packing up the house—it had been a month already since we'd moved, and we hadn't missed these items at all.

Our brand-new air purifier made a growling sound as we worked.

My sister and I were sitting on the frictionless, stepless expanse of our new apartment's floor, rummaging through boxes. "I can't believe we paid money to move this here!" my sister would say again and again, frustrated, as she pulled things out and put them directly in the garbage.

And it was true, we could have left a lot of this stuff there and saved on the moving costs. My sister calculated out some of the waste and got even more upset.

Nonetheless, we made progress this way until at last, almost everything had been unpacked. There was only one box left.

We opened it and my sister cried out with glee.

The box contained our mother's things from her room: used lipsticks and compacts, a desk lamp, balls of lace yarn, things like that. All carefully packed by my daughter, from the looks of it. My sister plunged her hands into the pile of lace yarn and pulled out a silver laptop she'd glimpsed buried underneath.

"We could sell this, I bet!"

Our mother had bought it quite a few years ago.

After Mitsuko's tax troubles, our mother's lacemaking classes were cancelled, and with the earthquake and tsunami, she got more and more into online life, starting with Facebook and LINE but gradually, in her hunt-and-peck way, mastering her computer and even beginning her own blog, which she called *Lacework Diary*.

Mother became obsessed, buying a high-end digital camera to take pictures of the doilies and vests she made to upload onto her blog. *Lacework Diary* never really took off in popularity, but it let her stay in contact with students who'd taken her classes, and she always got a kick out of it when someone she didn't know left a thumbs-up or an encouraging comment. She always made sure every comment received a thoughtful reply.

But ever since she broke her leg, she hadn't been able to complete a project, so the computer went into the closet and then eventually got packed up in this box. The digital camera seemed to be lost for good.

My sister rummaged around in the box until she came up with a white power cord. She plugged it into the wall and connected it to the computer on her lap. She pushed the power button with a finger still clad in a work glove.

"This must have cost a pretty penny when she bought it."

It certainly might have, but now it's years out of date—we'll be lucky if it turns on at all. I'd already turned back to look in the box again when I heard it chime.

Bahhhhn.

"Oh! It's booting up!"

Surprised, I slid in next to my sister and looked along with her at the screen.

The black surface of the monitor was suddenly illuminated by a flash of light.

As the computer came on, a prompt appeared, asking for a password. A cursor blinked inside a white rectangle.

My sister shook the work glove off her hand and tapped the keys. A row of dots appeared within the rectangle.

Incorrect password

The rectangle shivered, then went blank.

My sister thought for a moment, then tapped the keys once more. This time the password screen unlocked.

"Bingo!" said my sister, clenching her fists in victory as the start-up screen appeared. Mother's computer was coming back to life.

I was really impressed. I knew my sister worked in IT, but I hadn't realized she could unlock passwords like that. "Are you a hacker?" I asked, but my sister scoffed at me.

"As if!" she said. "All I did was think it over and then I made a guess! You could figure out what password Mother would use, too, if you thought about it a little."

The password had been her phone number.

The number for a phone that no longer existed, at a house that no longer did either.

"It makes me a little angry it was so easy, though—a weak password's no good, Mother!" My sister seemed sincerely upset about it.

The computer chimed and the desktop appeared on-screen.

Hearing it felt like when I heard the phone ring in the old house. It was like I was hearing it ring on and on, this old sound that no longer had any place in the world.

The desktop background was a close-up of a lace doily. The resolution wasn't very good, though, and parts of the image were pixelated.

My sister started opening up folders right away.

"What's this?" she murmured.

There was a file with the name "Diary."

Diary.

Diaries were things secreted away in laptops now, rather than under beds or pillows.

I took off my work gloves as well and settled in next to the computer.

"What are we going to do?"

My sister and I looked at each other, both of us still wearing masks.

"You want to take a look?" My sister asked this with utmost sincerity.

"We might find a love confession—an account of raw passion!"

Neither of us spoke for a few moments.

"What do you say? What if it's like *The Bridges of Madison County* or something?"

I laughed despite myself. "Stop—you're making me imagine it!"

"Imagine what—Mother with Clint Eastwood?"

We both cracked up at that.

Sobering slightly, my sister turned back to the computer and opened the file.

But what we read didn't keep us laughing.

It was no account of raw passion we'd found. If only it had been.

Sunday, July 16

All night I could hear the frogs in the nearby pond as they mated.

It was five a.m. The winds and thunder and rain had passed. It would be a clear dawn.

The men had their money out and were making wagers.

So, what will it be, boy or girl?

A dollar on boy.

A dollar on girl.

Money piled up on the table.

This was New Mexico, at the White Sands Proving Ground.

At Trinity, near Los Alamos.

It wasn't a woman with her legs spread at the center of that crowd of men, though, but rather a tall metal test tower.

Suspended on the tower was a metal orb, covered in cords and measuring 1.5 meters in diameter.

It was the Gadget. The world's first atomic bomb.

To bet on it being a boy or girl was to bet on the scope of the explosion.

But the most important bet was ten dollars on whether the blast would be born at all.

A man wearing a porkpie hat with a pipe gripped in his teeth held out a ten-dollar bill.

Ten dollars says it will be born.

The man had black hair and eyes the pale blue of mountain bellflower. The pale blue of ice.

His name was Robert. He was forty-one years old.

The flat, barren earth he stood upon was muddy beneath his feet.

It rained so little and was so dry, they sometimes had to brush their teeth with Coke in place of water.

Yet that day and that day only, a heavy rain had fallen.

The sandy mud turned red as the tips of his black leather shoes pressed into it. Despite the area being called White Sands.

Just nearby, in Alamogordo, the sand was gypsum and really was white, the dunes there dazzlingly so, as far as the eye could see.

The Skypilot *was playing on the radio.*

The countdown was beginning.

The men spread sunscreen on their faces.

Black sunglasses were handed out. Some men put them on, while others simply walked behind the glass shielding in front of the track.

Two minutes.

Robert said to himself under his breath: God, this is no good for my heart.

After all, it wasn't just his ten-dollar bet on the line if the birth miscarried. Two billion dollars would be down the drain as well.

One minute.

50 seconds.

40 seconds.

30 seconds.

20 seconds.

10

9

8

7

6

5

4

3

2

1

The Sky Pilot *ended, and music began to play.*

It was "Sunrise Serenade."

The music was by Frankie Carle, the lyrics by Jack Lawrence.

Glenn Miller and His Orchestra were playing it.

The Frankie Carle Orchestra version had been released earlier by the U.S. War Department as part of the V-Disc program, dropped by parachute along with phonographs around the world.

July 16, 1945, 05:29:45.

The gold leaf around the plutonium core blew apart as the bomb exploded.

Sunrise was to be at 06:53.

Leaving 1 hour, 23 minutes, and 15 seconds left to go.

Yet the area lit up brighter than midday.

Then a great rumbling boiled up from the ground.

I became light.

I stared at the screen, trembling.

My sister and I turned to look at each other.

"What *is* this?"

My sister began to look carefully at the file's digital information. It seemed it really had been created on Mother's computer.

Staring at the words didn't reveal anything, of course, as they were just data—there was no handwriting or ink smudges or any other evidence of authorship on the virtual page.

. . .

I STOOD UP suddenly, as if to push the computer away from me.

And I ran straight into our mother's new room in our new apartment.

The flooring was ridiculously slick, the veneer-covered plywood door weirdly lightweight.

I approached the electric bed and lifted the pillows, then rolled back the mat covering the mattress. I opened the hard-shell suitcase where we kept Mother's clothes for going to the day service and tipped it over onto the floor.

My sister, for her part, went straight for the claw-footed mahogany chest sitting in the corner. The chest had looked so elegant and expensive in the old house, but here it just looked old, a scuffed knockoff.

My sister pulled open the bottom drawer and grabbed the woolen skirts packed in there.

And that's when we saw it.

From the depths of the drawer, a green glass vase came out with the skirts and fell onto the floor.

That vase. That vase that should have been in the garbage and long gone by now. That vase that we took out of Father's study and put in the cinched-up bag that sat beneath the fig tree in the garden until it was carted away for good. There it was again, like a ghost.

But now that I really looked at it, I realized it wasn't the same vase—this one was much smaller, a mere bud vase. Digging through the rest of the drawer, more green glass items emerged: wine glasses, a necklace. Pulling out a scarf from the very back of the drawer, several small green glass beads fell out of it and rolled across the floor.

I realized, finally. All this glass was uranium glass!

I'd seen a show about it on TV. Uranium glass glowed fluorescent green under ultraviolet light, including light from the sun. All of the pieces scattered on the floor were glowing in the sunlight filtering into the room.

I picked up the garbage bag we'd been using and shoved all the glass into it.

My sister started ripping open the rest of the drawers in the room. In a kind of frenzy, I joined her.

We found a stack of lacy brassieres and girdles in a rainbow of colors.

And behind them, a stone. A shiny, black stone.

Black, like the darkest part of the night.

Black, like a curse.

I grabbed it with my hand

I felt its stillness, its cold weight.

I suddenly grew frightened. I felt a darkness, like a mysterious voice, entering my body from where my fingers closed over the stone's cold surface, and I screamed and threw it away from me onto the floor.

My sister quickly grabbed a pair of Mother's lavender lace underwear and used it to pick the accursed stone up and throw it in the garbage bag.

"Why does she have such fancy underwear, anyway? Gross."

This was my sister's only comment as she closed the top of the garbage bag and left to take it to the apartment building's trash collection area.

Yes, just throw it away.

Just get rid of it, throw it all away.

I leaned with my forehead against the window. All I could see was sky.

The trash collection area was inside the building on the first floor, so the garbage was now invisible, nowhere to be seen.

I was no longer haunted by that translucent bag staring at me day after day from beneath the fig tree.

It was all gone now. I didn't have to see any of it anymore.

WHEN SHE RETURNED, my sister and I proceeded to delete the "Diary" file from Mother's computer.

It took no more than a split second. All we had to do was drag and drop the file onto the garbage can icon, then press the button confirming the disposal. There was no trace left: a small chime sounded and then the file was gone, nowhere to be found.

Wordlessly, my sister and I folded the skirts and scarves and placed them back in the drawer in the mahogany chest. Then we remade the bed.

Not a cardboard box remained in the entire apartment.

It was all gone now: that house, the past itself. Gone without a trace.

I went to wash my hands in the bright white sink in the bathroom.

I passed my hands beneath the silver faucet.

An invisible force turned the faucet on, and water flowed out.

The mirror's surface was photocatalytic and would never rust or tarnish.

Yet no matter how much I washed my hands, I couldn't rid them of the feeling left behind by that accursed stone.

We must not let Mother out of our sight.

We must not let anyone know about what we read in that "Diary," or about what we found in the mahogany chest or anywhere else in her room.

My sister and I never let the word "Trinity" pass our lips again.

THAT NIGHT, MY sister and I made a thorough search of my mother's person when she returned from the day service. We laid her out on the bed, removed the beige underwear with her name written in them that we'd bought at the supermarket especially for her day-service trips. We even checked inside her genitals, an intrusion to which she, perhaps because she'd become so accustomed to others caring for her bodily needs, obediently acquiesced.

We discovered three uranium glass beads in the pocket of her elastic-cuffed sweatpants.

And we discovered that the computer we thought we'd sell, far from making us money, would actually cost us more to throw away.

DAYTIME

The physicist can tell very precisely how long it will take a gram of radium to lose half its radioactivity, but he absolutely can't say when a single atom of that radium will decay. If a man heads toward a fork in the road, and doesn't take the one to the left, it's obvious that he'll take the one to the right; but our choices are almost never between two alternatives alone. Every choice is followed by others, all multiple, and so on into infinity; and, finally, our future also depends heavily on external factors, completely extraneous to our deliberate choices, and on internal factors, of which we are not aware. For these obvious reasons, we can't know our own future or that of our neighbor; for the same reasons, no one can say what his past would have been "if."

—Primo Levi, *If This Is a Man* (1947)

12:00

☆ WELCOME!!! ☆
☆ To Re: Re: Re:'s Room! ☆

I heard there once was a forest on the premises of the Fukushima Dai-ichi Nuclear Power Plant. It was called the Forest of Wild Birds.

Several times a year, they would open the forest to the public, and families would come and have fun. Young and old alike would spread out blue plastic tarps on the grass and view the mountain cherries.

They would bring box lunches filled with all sorts of goodies: sandwiches filled with tuna or egg salad or jam, rice balls filled with salmon or pickled plum, pieces of fried chicken, meatballs.

Countless white clover blossoms were plucked and woven into crowns. Mountain rhododendron bloomed vivid crimson, while white tufts of lily-of-the-valley sprang up beside the mochi trees.

As summer turned into autumn, the pampas grass and fleabane would be covered in flowers like cottony clouds. Bellflowers of pale lavender could be glimpsed in the shade beneath the trees. The forest floor would be covered with so many fallen chestnuts and acorns that you could never gather them all!

And no matter the season, the forest would be filled with birdsong.

Which is surely how the Forest of Wild Birds got its name.

Of course, that wasn't its official name. It's just what everyone from the area, including the Tokyo Electric people, called it.

Takagi-san, the man I sat next to on the bus during the field trip, was the one who told me about the forest. What kind of birds were singing there? I wondered. But I forgot to ask! (TДT)

Takagi-san had moved to this area when he got married, and he raised his children here, made a life. But now he's never coming back—in fact, he can't.

The Forest of Wild Birds was cut down and the area turned into a space filled with holding tanks for contaminated water. I looked outside through the windows of the nine-story prefab building they set up on the premises—it can hold up to 1200 people! I saw a landscape filled with cranes and rows of enormous holding tanks extending all the way to the ocean. My heart grew full at the sight.

Along one side of the tanks, there was a single row of cherry trees—the only trees that hadn't been cut down. Their branches were covered in fresh pink blossoms.

☆

Nonetheless, I found the landscape there fascinating—so mysterious and dreamlike. There were no trees or flowers at all. Only a flat, silvery expanse extending in all directions, as far as the eye could see.

I was told the reason for this was that vegetation provides surfaces for radioactive material to cling to, raising radiation levels in the whole area. So, they cut down all the trees, and to prevent grass from growing, they decided to cover the ground with silvery cement. The areas where you had to wear hazmat suits were reduced considerably due to this measure.

I was so surprised—on the field trip, we were told we didn't have to wear hazmat suits or even masks! We were just given APD radiation detectors (pocket dosimeters outfitted with alarms) and cotton gloves. Dressed like that, we sat in the bus on seats covered in plastic sheets and looked out the window at the Dai-ichi tower—the one that exploded, whose iron skeleton was exposed in the blast.

That was the one area that seemed to have high radiation levels, and Takagi-san's Geiger counter went off as we drove through it. Everywhere else seemed fine, though, and his Geiger counter remained quiet for the rest of the trip.

(By the way, they told us we couldn't bring cameras or phones onto the premises—so no pictures for this post! Only Geiger counters were allowed. So sorry ☹)

☆

Everywhere was so clean and organized and brightly lit, it was like being in a huge convenience store. It's true! They even had an actual convenience store there—last year, a Lawson opened up in the prefab building.

We ate our lunch all together in the prefab building's cafeteria. The building was where the workers decommissioning the nuclear facility took their breaks, so there were always lots of people there. ♡ There were so many young handsome guys. ♡

The food was brought in from the Fukushima Revitalization Meal Service Center, located about nine kilometers away in the Ōkawara District of Ōkuma. We toured the Meal Service Center too—there were a lot of women working there. And they weren't washing the rice or preparing it for steaming. The rice was cooked at the push of a single button. They told us they could make meals for up to 3,000 people at a time!

On the menu that day, we could choose from two kinds of rice bowls, a noodle dish, and a curry meal. I personally chose the fried chicken set meal with grated daikon and deep-fried tofu with vegetables. It only cost ¥380!

♫It was so-o go-od!♫

BY THE TIME I looked up at the clock on the wall after scrolling all the way to the bottom of Re:'s blog, I saw it read exactly 12:00 p.m.

Re:'s blog had flashing pink and yellow stars scattered throughout, lighting up the monitor in front of me. I made sure to hit Sleep to make the screen go dark before I stood up from my desk.

At the desk across from mine, Michiyo and Taki were eating their lunches—a bento box and an aluminum foil-wrapped sandwich, respectively—in front of a computer that was showing the

Olympic torch relay. No one else seemed to be around, and the office, with only half its lights turned on, seemed much emptier than usual.

Taki looked up from the computer and, still chewing his sandwich, said to me, "Are you looking for Tomi and Lee?"

Michiyo used the pink plastic chopsticks gripped between her barnacle-nailed fingers to point out the window. "They said they were going to that organic ¥500 lunch place on the corner, if you want to join them!"

I was in the midst of a noncommital response when I felt a warm, bloody mass let loose from between my legs; I hurried to the bathroom.

RE:'S GRANDMOTHER HAD made the news on the first Friday in July, two weeks before I'd arrived at her blog, by committing a terrorist act. This was three months after the incident with the old man who said he was from Sankt Joachimsthal, and two months after we'd found Mother's "Diary."

The Olympics were about to start, finally, and the news was about nothing else—anything unpleasant had been pushed out of sight, forgotten. Although, looking back, this was clearly just the quiet before the storm. From that day onward, I was no longer able to get a good night's sleep again.

A typhoon had moved north through the Japanese mainland that day, and it had been raining since morning. Michiyo and Taki were huddled in front of a computer together like always, eating their lunches while watching the torch relay.

"It's tough having to run in all that rain, poor guy."

Michiyo was making her usual caustic remarks as she ate her bento, while Taki was pointing out how you could see a male runner's nipples through his wet tank top.

Perhaps because of the typhoon raging, almost everyone seemed to be packed in the office. It was stiflingly humid despite the air-conditioning, and everything outside looked gloomy and dark.

I went to the break area, mixed my green smoothie powder into my soy milk and drank it. I'd just rinsed out the plastic shaker at the sink and returned to my desk when it happened.

There was a small crowd gathered now around Michiyo and Taki.

Everyone was peering at the computer.

Was it some famous idol's turn today or something? I walked around so I could see the monitor too.

And indeed, I saw on the screen that someone was running.

Running beneath a white ceiling of clouds.

It was a parking lot at a suburban mall somewhere.

Someone was sprinting straight across the parking lot. An old person. A woman.

But it was no torch relay.

Instead, she carried a black, shiny stone in her hand.

A Trinity!

I felt my breath catch in my throat.

My fingertips grew cold, remembering the feel of the accursed stone.

Taguchi, her belly swollen and about to go on maternity leave, was standing next to me, her eyes wide.

"She's really quite a runner, isn't she?"

The old woman, her sensible white bob in disarray, was sprinting along dressed in a white tank top and bright-red shorts. Her limbs may have been desiccated from age and her shoes just beat-up old Adidas, but her back was straight, her form perfect.

For a moment—just a moment—I thought it was Mother.

I thought she had given the day service the slip and ran away to the other side of the screen, and I got chills.

But of course, as soon as I took a good look at this woman, I realized she looked nothing like my mother, and besides, her leg wouldn't even let her walk right now, much less run like that.

Taki's voice was filled with excitement as he said, "We should ask her to be the spokeswoman for our new water-purifier campaign!"

"Make up some presentation materials and we'll have a look," replied Tomi, in seeming earnestness as she fixed one of the many pins in her hair, causing a bit of laughter.

But soon everyone was quiet again, transfixed by what was unfolding.

The footage was a livestream. A flow of comments from other users ran down the side of the image.

A Trinity's decided to run a one-woman torch relay!

What a wonderful opening for the One-Woman Olympics!

The Olympics are, of course, a festival of peace.

This is a terrorist attack—everyone get away, right now!

It's happening!!!!!!! ~~~(°∀°)~~~!!!!!

According to the comments, we were looking at a mall in the town of Tomioka in Futaba, not far from the Fukushima Dai-ichi nuclear plant. In fact, it was within the twenty-kilometer mandatory evacuation radius, but the evacuation order had been lifted three years ago, on the first of April 2017.

"Is that really Fukushima?" Lee murmured to herself as she watched the feed.

The old woman was running past a line of banners.

As we watched the livestream, Taki took out his tablet and started looking for information about what was happening. Michiyo heaved herself into position to look over his shoulder.

The sound of the falling rain resounded through the office. Water fell in ropes from the sky outside the windows.

The tablet gripped in Taki's hands was showing a grainy video of some kind.

The side of a building painted in blue-and-white ocean camouflage was partly torn down, its iron skeleton exposed. A red-and-white-striped crane stood nearby. The actual ocean peeked out from behind the building; its surface glittered, reflecting the light of the sun.

A dark silhouette was running down the road leading up to it.

Michiyo grabbed at the tablet to try to look closer, asking, "Where is that?"

Taki enlarged the picture.

"It's the live feed of a security camera at the Fukushima Daiichi Nuclear Power Station Number One."

. . .

ACCORDING TO TAKI, the old woman had been part of a tour of the Fukushima Dai-ichi Nuclear Power Plant facilities; she'd gotten off the bus partway through the tour and started running straight for Power Station Number One.

She was discovered trying to get into the power station building by hazmat-suited workers. She dashed away from them, but they caught up with her as she was attempting to scramble up a pile of bags filled with contaminated soil. She fought back with the accursed stone in her hand, hitting the men with it and escaping again. Eventually, she carjacked a truck, incapacitating the driver and taking him as a hostage as she led a chase that brought her near the Futaba police station in Tomioka before running into an electric pole.

She jumped out of the truck, stripped off her long-sleeved shirt and long pants and ran away, dressed as she was now.

The suspect was Kiyoko Himeno, age ninety-one.

Everyone gasped involuntarily when they heard the age.

Ninety-one !

The whole office was soon alive with murmuring conversations.

"Well there was that British-Indian lady, Fauja Singh—she ran a full marathon at a hundred, right?"

"This lady should qualify to join the Olympics!"

The workers who tried to chase her down sustained injuries that would keep them in the hospital for a week. The driver she'd taken hostage was out for another two.

"She's strong, too—let's sign her up for the shot put as well!" said Michiyo when she heard the woman had assaulted the men so effectively.

Everyone laughed at that.

The sound of the rain intensified again, momentarily drowning out the sound of the laughter.

Taki continued to search for details, but the nuclear facility had put a lockdown on information and the only photos available were two distributed by Tokyo Electric.

One showed a pile of large black sacks full of contaminated soil and the old woman crawling up it on all fours like a frog. The second showed her from behind, running full tilt through a vast silver plain.

Michiyo took the tablet out of Taki's hands and used her fingers to enlarge the photos, scrutinizing them by holding them first far away, then close up, to her face. Was she farsighted?

"Is this some kind of photoshop? It looks like a shot from a near-future sci-fi thing."

"The ground is silver?"

And it did seem that the old woman was running through a landscape that was nothing but an endless silver plain.

Taki's tablet was passed from person to person to peruse. People enlarged and miniaturized the photo to their heart's content, but no one had an explanation for why the ground was silver. It was only after I'd read Re:'s blog two weeks later that I learned that the reactor premises had been covered in silvery cement to prevent vegetation from attracting and retaining radiation.

On the far side of the screen, the old woman continued to run.

The totally ordinary mall parking lot was still being shown. A middle-aged woman was packing shopping bags filled with toilet paper and green onions into her white minivan.

Taguchi rubbed her belly absently with one hand, frowning.

"It's weird it's so normal-looking inside the twenty-kilometer evacuation zone, isn't it?"

Tomi nodded in agreement.

"I'd pictured it as a bunch of ruins."

In the parking lot on the far side of the screen, two guys in T-shirts and shorts who seemed to have just happened by right then had their phones out, filming the running woman.

"I'd imagined that in the evacuation zone, you'd have to wear a hazmat suit, or you'd die," murmured Michiyo.

The comment stream on the side of the livestream was now filled with screenshots from the Twitter account of the running woman.

It's not me who suffers from true memory loss. It's all of you—you who fail to remember the past, you who cannot feel even the tiniest bit of the pain of that which cannot be seen.

Rain began to fall even on the other side of the screen. The asphalt of the parking lot gradually blackened, as if the rain were falling ink. The young men draped towels over their heads and ran toward their car. The running woman's beat-up sneakers began to absorb rainwater and turn black too. Every time her feet hit the ground, water would fly up in the air.

The sound of the rain outside the windows resounded throughout the office. The rain was continuing out there, too, it seemed. It made me uneasy.

The place where the old woman was running was supposed to be completely separate from here, a land far distant from the one where I lived, with no relation or connection binding us together. Yet a single typhoon was dropping rain both here and there as it made its way slowly up the island.

If making visible the suffering and anguish of the invisible is terrorism, then call me a terrorist.

This is the beginning of the revenge of the invisible.

The old woman had reached the edge of the parking lot and was about to run out into the road beyond.

The camera following her swung around wildly and ended up focusing on the rusted sign of the long-closed conveyor-belt sushi place on the other side of the road. Raindrops fell on the lens and ran in streaks down the image.

Suddenly, the image broadened and cleared up.

A white expanse of sky came into view.

Michiyo, clutching the tablet she'd stolen from Taki, yelled, "Is that *Disneyland*?"

And indeed, there beneath the white sky, there were three pastel-colored buildings in a row that wouldn't look out of place in Disneyland. In front of them were round patches of neatly trimmed lawn. A little wooden bench ringed the base of a tree. One building had walls painted light grey and peppermint green with white-trimmed windows, while the one next to it was pale yellow with arched doorways. A small clock tower topped with a weather vane separated the yellow one from the last one, which was red brick with a black roof. There was even an old-fashioned gas-powered lamppost in front.

It made us doubt our own eyes—like something out of a fantasy movie.

But it was clear that this was still Tomioka, a city within the twenty-kilometer evacuation zone.

The old woman, with her sinewy legs, jumped lightly over the low fence and began running toward the courtyard in front of the buildings. Her wet red running shorts were unsettlingly eye-catching.

Comments appeared along the side of the image.

Where is that?

What are those buildings? A mirage?

This is too surreal!

It turned out that these buildings were formerly the Energy Museum—now repurposed as the TEPCO Decommissioning Archive Center—that had been created to facilitate public relations for the Fukushima Dai-ni Nuclear Power Station. Commenters posted photos from Tokyo Electric's website and from brochures touting the place as a tourist destination. It seemed they were replicas of the homes of Albert Einstein, Marie Curie, and Thomas Edison, constructed as a line of continuous buildings.

Back when it was the Energy Museum, it apparently had an anime-themed bakery-slash-café attached to it that was a popular spot for mothers to bring their daughters. Business hours had been from nine-thirty a.m. to four-thirty p.m., and the museum had closed every third Sunday. Admission had been free.

Michiyo took a photo of the screen with her smartphone, saying, “I thought I was hallucinating!”

The old woman was heading straight for the Decommissioning Archive Center.

Her white hair, drenched in the rain, stuck to her forehead and cheeks, and water ran down her face. As we watched, she reached the arched doorway of the pale-yellow building—that is, the one modeled on Marie Curie’s home. Police in black rain jackets emerged from behind Thomas Edison’s house and raced toward her.

A mother and child stood next to the entrance to the archive center, rooted to the spot as they watched the scene unfold.

The police drew closer to the old woman.

The old woman wielded the black stone in her hand with authority.

As she did, she pounded on the door to Marie Curie’s house.

The camera was too far from the scene to pick up the sound of the old woman’s words or her pounding on the door.

It just silently showed her as she banged on the door again and again.

Taguchi brought her hands to her mouth and stomach simultaneously.

Tomi audibly sucked in her breath.

Everyone grew silent.

The same line was posted over and over in the comments running down the side of the screen.

> **This is the beginning of the revenge of the invisible.**
>
> **This is the beginning of the revenge of the invisible.**
>
> **This is the beginning of the revenge of the invisible.**

Yet, the door would not open.

No matter how she pounded on it, there was no response.

It may have even been a false door, just a façade on a wall.

Unopenable, a door only in appearance.

The police swarmed around the old woman, surrounding her.

In the end, the old woman was tackled and arrested in front of Marie Curie's door.

The rainwater on the asphalt splashed up in the air as it happened.

The accursed stone dropped from her grip and rolled across the ground.

The camera swung around again, briefly showing the green-roofed clock tower.

And then just the white sky. Raindrops fell directly onto the lens.

The livestream cut off there. The image disappeared, and the screen filled with darkness.

. . .

WITHIN HOURS OF her arrest, it came out that this suspect, Kiyoko Himeno, experienced the same delusion as Tani, the other suspect—that she had been buried deep within the earth near Sankt Joachimsthal as well.

I lay deep beneath the earth, in darkness.

Until one day I was dug out, brought up into the light of the sun—only to be thrown away into a thickly wooded pine forest.

But then, one day, men came to the forest and picked me—picked us*—back up.*

We were gathered together and brought down the mountain to a station at the foot of a hill topped by a church. We were loaded onto a train.

How far did that train take us?

The place where we arrived was a city called Paris, in a country called France.

We were piled in the garden behind the ESPCI—L'École supérieure de physique et de chimie industrielles—not far from the Panthéon.

There was a full ton of us—a small mountain of accursed stones.

And a few pine needles, too, from the forests of Sankt Joachimsthal.

A woman came and picked one of us up, her eyes shining. They were pale grey.

The woman was named Marie.

Marie Curie. She was thirty-two years old, preparing the thesis that would earn her her doctorate.

She was joined by her husband, Pierre. Together they washed us, smashed us to pieces, heated us up, stored us in a nearby shed.

The shed stank of death. For it had been previously used by the medical school to perform autopsies.

More and more accursed stones were brought from Sankt Joachimsthal to join us.

In the end, nearly eleven tons in all.

And from us, there was made 0.1 grams of something entirely new.

Something that released enormous amounts of radiation.

I—that is, we*—gave off light. A pale blue phosphorescence.*

We radiated *it. A Latin root that gave us our new name:* Radium.

We had been despised, called accursed.

But now, that which had been drawn from us was one of the most valuable materials in the world—more valuable than silver, more valuable than gold.

The price of a single gram of radium was 750,000 francs.

Marie called us "fairy lights," and kept us next to her bed, beside her pillow.

Marie and Pierre won the Nobel Prize but were unable to attend the ceremony.

Marie had been pregnant with a baby girl but ended up miscarrying, and she began to sleepwalk, wandering her room at night as Pierre writhed and cried out in pain from rheumatoid arthritis.

Yet news of radium's discovery had spread around the world—everyone wanted us!

Radium could cure cancer, they said.

This was the beginning of radiation therapy.

But no one, no matter how rich, could get their hands on us.

For no one knew of another place besides Sankt Joachimsthal where they could find us.

The rich became obsessed, and devoted themselves to searching for other sources of radium.

They began to focus their attentions on the springs that bubbled up from deep in the earth of Sankt Joachimsthal.

For their waters contained traces of radium and were radioactive.

Rumors began to spread far and wide.

If you drank of these springs, or submerged your body in them, your cancer would be cured.

Not just cancer, but all sorts of ailments—rheumatism, dysentery, so many things.

Because these springs were radium springs.

And, so, we became a miracle, a medical miracle.

The rich came from all over Europe to Sankt Joachimsthal.

The townspeople poured the water into barrels, used it to brew "radium beer" and bake "radium bread."

Soon enough, a grand hotel opened that became known as the Radium Palace.

It was the world's first radium spa hotel. It was a gorgeous five-story structure designed by an architect from Vienna, capital of the Austro-Hungarian Empire. Beneath it, there was a ballroom; beside it, in the forest, a tennis court.

But why would we know all this?

Because we visited it once. Marie brought us.

We visited the earth from which we'd originally come. Through the Palace window, we glimpsed the pine forests of Sankt Joachimsthal into which we'd once been discarded.

It was June 16, 1925.

Marie wore a round hat tied with a wide ribbon, and a voluminous, wide-sleeved overcoat.

A huge crowd had gathered in Sankt Joachimsthal to welcome her.

With a burst of magnesium, a commemorative photograph was taken.

Marie's eyes were open for the flash, but, due to her cataracts, she barely saw it.

THIS WAS THE story told and retold by Kiyoko Himeno after her arrest. While she had apparently graduated from elementary school, she could not read or write Japanese and had no history of travel overseas or of learning any other language, and she'd been confined to a nursing home prior to the incident. It was still being investigated how she could have learned the information now spilling forth from her.

Returning home after work that day on the Saikyō Line, caught in the crush of rush hour, I read all the articles on the internet I could find. The rain had continued thanks to the typhoon, so the air inside the train car was humid and fetid-smelling from everyone's wet umbrellas and clothes.

I saw that the first suspect, Tani, whose name meant *valley*, had been nicknamed Saint Joachim's Valley, while Himeno, whose name included the character for *princess*, earned the moniker Radium Princess.

People were talking about the possibility that it had all been part of the Radium Princess's plan to be arrested at the door to Marie Curie's home.

The Radium Princess asked how it was that Marie Curie had accomplished such an unprecedented, monumental task.

She had already theorized the existence of a radioactive material like radium well before she actually discovered it. But when she presented her findings, her fellow scientists refuted the possibility out of hand.

If you say you don't know its atomic mass, that's the same as saying it doesn't exist!

Show us this so-called "radium," then we might believe you!

For them, a new element could only be said to exist after it had been seen, touched, weighed, investigated, exposed to various acids, inserted into a flask, its atomic mass determined. Radium, at that point, had been seen by *no one.*

And, so, Marie decided.

She would show them—she would render the invisible visible.

Since that's what it would take to prove its existence to those who claimed that being unseen, unfelt, and unmeasured was the same as not being at all.

THE WET UMBRELLA of the woman standing in front of me in the train pressed against my legs, soaking my navy-blue pants. I pushed the umbrella away and continued scrolling on my phone.

I clicked on photos of the Radium Palace that I found in a gallery on an aggregator website, enlarging each one.

The Radium Palace, located in Saint Joachim's valley, now Jáchymov, in the Czech Republic.

The world's first radium-spring spa. Opened in 1912. According to Booking.com, a night there cost ¥14,798.

Photos of the hotel's entrance were culled by internet commentators from tourism sites and pored over. A black-and-white photograph of Marie Curie on the wall beneath a chandelier was circled in red, an arrow drawn to it. The text of the plate beneath it had been run through machine translation and posted beneath the photo.

Two-time Nobel Prize—winner Marie Curie—the venerated scientist who succeeded in extracting the world's first radioactive material, radium, from *pitchblende* (accursed stone; scientific name: uraninite) excavated from Saint Joachim's Valley here in Jáchymov—visited our city on June 16, 1925, and stayed at this hotel.

There were other photos: a huge, gilt-framed mirror; a bathrobe featuring an embroidered *RP* monogram; a cocktail called Radium Palace that was red as fresh blood; a sculpture on the patio of a woman bearing a ring of light upon her back.

I swiped through the photos of this distant place, trembling.

Looking at them, my mother's previous visit was thrust before me in newly visible form, filling me with unease.

The website informed me that the radium-spring boom had also come to Japan, and that there had even been a time when the radium springs near Iizaka, in Fukushima Prefecture, were so popular that a special train line had been set up to bring people there; internet commentators were now speculating on possible connections between this and the current terrorism. In the margin of the web page were pictures showing a cartoon character based on Iizaka's famous "radium eggs" cooked in the hot-spring water and an anime-inspired caricature of the author Mori Ogai, who had conducted surveys in his capacity as surgeon general of the Japanese Army under his real name, Mori Rintarō, to assess how much radium was contained in Japan's hot springs.

The internet was abuzz with speculation.

Was this just the first step in a master plan by the Trinities to spread terror across the country?

Would even more hideous acts be perpetrated at their hands?

Was the next target the Olympic torch relay? The Opening Ceremony?!

I looked up from my phone and saw a middle-aged man in a suit standing right in front of me, sweat running down his forehead as he voraciously scrolled through his phone. Sneaking a peek at his screen, I saw that it was aglow with gaudy neon pink and yellow stars—Re:'s blog.

Re:—the granddaughter of suspected terrorist Himeno, the Radium Princess.

Looking around the internet, I saw people accusing Re: of having instigated the Radium Princess's actions. A web page spelled it out in huge red Gothic letters: ***Re: is the real terrorist!*** The same website published her email address, physical address, phone number, and even a picture of the elementary school she'd attended.

We cannot forgive Re:'s violent acts! We must restore peace to Japan!

On the way back to my high-rise from the train station, I passed two flags, one showing the Olympic rings against a blue-and-white-checked background and the other showing the Olympic mascot: a pink robot from the near future. They drooped motionless, drenched by the heavy rain.

The mascot supposedly had the power to move things just by looking at them.

But even it lacked the power to move what could not be seen.

THAT NIGHT, AS was my habit now, I inspected my mother's body—every nook and cranny, every crease and orifice—then put her in her pajamas and laid her in her adjustable bed. I massaged her swollen, dry-skinned legs, smearing them with heparinoid cream. I called my daughter into the room, and we each took one of my mother's feet and helped her do her physical therapy exercises, moving each leg backward and forward. My daughter had her earbuds in all the while.

My eyes popped open again and again all through the night. Or more likely, I just never properly fell sleep in the first place.

Tossing and turning in the brand-new bed I'd bought when I moved in, I stared in the shadowy gloom at the pattern embossed on the white-on-white wallpaper.

There was no rose pattern, no framed photograph, no big black stain behind it.

And outside the window: no fig tree, no garbage bag, nothing.

All that was there on the far side of the glass was rain falling soundlessly in the dark.

The garbage had been hauled away; the data deleted.

Unable to sleep, I picked up my phone, which was still tethered to the wall by its power cord.

I began to search.

Trinity

Before I knew it, I'd entered the same word again and again into the search window.

Trinity, Trinity, Trinity

The phone's LCD glow was the only light in the room.

I read everything I could about the Trinity disease and the old people afflicted with it.

I checked through the Trinity Self-Check List.

- You find yourself lost while taking a road you've taken many times before.
- You cannot remember what you ate for breakfast.
- You reflexively pick up rocks you find lying on the ground.

I kept checking through these lists until I got to a result that said Mom hadn't turned Trinity.

I kept searching.

Trinity

I entered the characters into the window again and again like the words of a prayer.

Trinity, Trinity, Trinity

In Christianity, there are the three divine persons of God: Father, Son, and Holy Ghost.

But Google was no God and offered me no solace for my troubles.

Trinity

The name of the testing site at White Sands, New Mexico, where the first nuclear bomb was detonated.

Trinity

And then, finally, after traveling the internet looking at all these different Trinities, I found myself looking at one in particular.

A cybersex site.

Trinity

"Cybersex" sounded like something out of *The Matrix,* but the site itself was drab, just an inverted golden triangle in the center of a plain background.

It reminded me of the shape made by a woman's ovaries connecting to her uterus.

Thirty days free if you sign up now!

12:30

The bathroom I ran into from the office was deathly quiet. The young women I worked with, who were usually in here fixing their make up, were nowhere to be found. I was working during the holiday, after all, and besides, it was lunchtime. The only other woman in the office at the moment was Michiyo.

Sitting on the toilet, I looked down between my legs and saw that the pad I'd bought at the train station convenience store earlier was soaked with blood. Sighing, I unpeeled the pad and removed my tampon, setting them on the floor with one hand while getting out my phone with the other.

An unseen force unlocked my phone like a key unlatching a door, and my browser home page appeared.

I searched *Re:*.

A photo came up showing a dimly lit apartment with yellowing floors and walls. The living room was only six mats in size, the kitchen only two. The open closet was filled with meticulously organized clothes and miscellaneous plastic daily necessities, and the futon was still unrolled on the tatami. On top of the futon, placed in a circle, was a series of square silver objects—Re:'s "artwork"—and a shiny black stone. In the background, brightly colored bras and panties were hung out to dry on a plastic hanger for all to see.

Mystery Circle!!!!

It's not even the Heisei Period anymore,
but they still live like it's Showa???

These were the types of comments people left beneath this photo, which showed the apartment Re: shared with her grandmother, the Radium Princess.

According to these commentators, Re: and the Radium Princess had shared this apartment on the west side of their town before the police and mass media descended upon it. It seemed left over from another time amid the newly constructed homes surrounding it. Re: lived with her grandmother in this room on the first floor, laying their futons beside each other every night for upward of ten years.

Re:—real name Makoto Himeno, age forty-one—had quit her temp job to care for her grandmother, and was living mainly on her grandmother's pension and government assistance.

> Look at her, stealing her grandmother's welfare money, making that garbage she calls "art" and pushing her grandmother toward terrorism!
>
> Re: should be arrested as an accomplice!

There was comment after comment like this. Sitting on the toilet, I searched out these pages denouncing Re: and read them all, one after the other.

> Quitting your job to care for your family—what a wimp! And so rude to those who work hard to do both!
>
> Taking the blood and sweat of taxpayers and using it to make "art"! She should give that money back, and have all welfare taken from her!
>
> If she needed money, all she had to do was sell her body (she already has the right bras ♡).
>
> It's proof of her irresponsibility that she let that old terrorist run wild on her own!
>
> Nothing but gross negligence.
>
> Her existence itself is a problem. Die! Make amends by dying!

The criticism of Re: was intense. Several commenters threatened to kill her outright. There were rumors she was really Korean or Chinese—even Jewish.

I rummaged through the piles of slander.

A word balloon had been added to a photoshopped picture of Re: and turned into a GIF. Inside the balloon, cutesy characters:

Who eternally wills evil
and eternally works good?
♡ That is me—I am she! ♡

Filled with terror and excitement, I couldn't stop reading.

Blood continued to drip steadily from between my legs into the toilet as I scrolled.

Finally, I wiped my crotch with toilet paper and stood up.

A sensor made the toilet flush as if an unseen force had pressed a button, and my 342nd unfertilized egg, along with the 342nd unused uterine lining my body had created to nurture that egg, swirled down into the toilet's dark mouth, and disappeared.

She quit her job!

She was living on her relative's pension and welfare!

And that relative became a terrorist!

The more I criticized Re: in my head, the more my panic subsided.

This kind of thing could only happen to a person like Re:!

Re: and I are completely different kinds of people!

Re: just didn't try hard enough!

It's natural for someone like Re: to receive so much criticism and abuse!

In my heart, I joined the unseen crowd and spit on Re:, threw stones at her. I crucified her.

I opened Re:'s blog, went to her profile page, and tapped her self-portrait. She was wearing a puff-sleeved blouse patterned with stars and a black miniskirt, and she had a neon-pink band in her hair. She was looking down at the camera, her eyes fringed with disturbingly long fake lashes. Her age was listed as "40+" and her occupation was, naturally, "artist."

Looking at the photo, I laughed at her, looked down on her, and felt my uneasy heart grow calm.

For I believed that this woman, this Re:, was *a completely different type of person than me.*

As feelings of self-confidence swelled within me, I tapped on one of the thumbnails in the gallery section of her blog.

Welcome to Re: Re: Re:'s Gallery!

The screen filled with an image of one of the silvery "pieces" created by Re:, the self-proclaimed artist.

It was a series called *Landscape: 1F. 1F* referred not to the first floor of a building, but to the Fukushima Dai-ichi Nuclear Power Plant. According to the explanation, canvas was too expensive, so she applied the acrylic paint directly onto wooden panels.

By all appearances, the wood was covered with an uninterrupted coat of silver paint, but according to the description, under the silver paint was another painting, this one of a wildflower. Not just any flower, either—one of the flowers that had grown in the Forest of Wild Birds once found on the premises of the Dai-ichi plant.

In fact, each piece was named after a piece of vegetation that had once grown in the forest: *Lawn Grass, Common Fleabane, Cat's Ear, Lovegrass, Cudweed, Japanese Clover, Pampas Grass, Mugwort, Fever Vine, Gooseneck Loosestrife, Red Pine, Mountain Clover, Cat's Clover, Horsetail, Chinese Clover, Sparrow's Woodrush, Shady Clubmoss, Goldenrod, Bloodgrass, Wild Soybean, Mare's Tail, Crabgrass, Daisy Fleabane, White Clover . . .*

Each one was painted over with silver; each one looked exactly the same.

It seemed this was meant to simulate the landscape created by the eradication of all vegetation when the nuclear power reactor grounds were covered with silvery cement to reduce radiation levels.

So what? I read several comments making fun of Re:'s art.

She's a radiation idiot. A rad-iot! I saw this joke repeated everywhere, even on TV.

I imagined Re: in her tiny apartment, sitting on her futon, frowning in concentration as she drew these flowers that no longer exist.

She posted pictures of her process, and indeed, each piece at one point featured flowers painted in a bright, Pop Art style, full of neon pinks and yellows. But in the end, each and every one ended up covered over in silver, becoming seemingly identical monochrome canvases.

Scrolling down to the bottom, I saw that Re: had left a comment of her own.

THIS IS ME, Re:, and this is where I've been working hard on my ***Landscape: 1F*** series all this time! ♫

When the accident at the nuclear reactor happened, we were all inundated with pictures and videos: people dressed in hazmat suits; sidewalks and cobblestones with vegetation growing up through it, breaking it apart; livestock slowly starving to death; abandoned houses turning back into wild places like the Forest of Wild Birds; ostriches and boars running loose.

Of course, I saw these images too.

I saw them, and my heart hurt.

All the things we saw—they really existed.

And that we all saw them—that's also a fact.

But I noticed something.

I noticed that the one thing we didn't see was radiation.

It didn't appear in any photos or on TV. Just like what's inside our hearts.

And so, I asked myself, why do we want to see these images?

I asked myself, how can we look at them and know that they are, in fact, showing us a city polluted by radiation?

We look at these images and our hearts grow sad, we feel fear and outrage, we feel sympathy.

And yet, at the same time, didn't we also feel relieved?

Relieved because these places were not our places, these cities were not our cities.

No matter how ruined or pitiful these places appeared.

We looked at them because we wanted to confirm that they were somewhere else, distant from us, didn't we?

And in this way, we saw what we wanted to see, and even derived a certain satisfaction from it, didn't we?

And further, by doing this, we got the feeling that we'd seen everything there was to see, did we not?

And soon enough, we stopped doing even that, didn't we? We stopped looking, and began even to forget what we had seen?

And so, in these pieces, even though it's such a small thing, really, I decided to paint each flower in as fine a detail as possible, as methodically as possible—some of these paintings took a month to complete!

JUST AS I *suspected—she's crazy.* Murmuring this to myself, I turned off my phone. It made an audible *click* as the screen turned black.

I slammed the shiny black object onto the toilet paper dispenser as if thrusting it from myself and stood up from the toilet.

What does she expect people to see in these paintings showing nothing?

I looked behind myself, still half-crouched. I couldn't calm the disquiet growing in my chest.

There were pouches left by other female employees lined up on the shelf behind me. I reached into a black nylon one and withdrew a brand-new pad and tampon. I slipped the tampon into myself like a relay runner accepting a torch.

I used my fingertips to roll the blood-soaked pad and tampon up into the used tampon's plastic casing, and then wrapped the whole thing in toilet paper.

I opened up the plastic box in the corner of the stall and saw there were already used pads and tampons inside. Which meant there was at least one other woman in the office who had her period. Tomi-chan said she used reusable cloth napkins, so it must've been someone else. Michiyo and Lee were behaving as they always did, going about their work like normal, yet one of them may've been dripping blood from between her legs right this minute. Feeling a sense of strange solidarity, I placed my toilet paper—wrapped bundle atop the one already in the box and closed the lid.

My phone sat on the toilet paper holder, its screen showing nothing but darkness.

But the silver *Landscape: 1F* paintings still lingered in my mind.

That dark spring nine years ago.

The summer that followed, when the cicadas went silent.

Come to think of it, Sasaki's grandfather died soon after we'd seen him walking down the road with the stone.

Why should I be forced to confront these bitter memories from so long ago?

Why must I dig these things back up that should have been thrown out, forgotten, buried deep in the ground?

I rose up slightly from the toilet seat and pulled my underwear, along with the new pad I'd stuck inside it, snug against my vagina. Everything in place, I sat back down and picked up my phone, staring into its screen once more.

I navigated back to the Trinity site and started typing.

<< I'm horny again

<< I'm touching myself now, imaging you licking my pussy

<< You must be especially good at that, right? With a name like Cerberus ?

I tried adding a dog emoji to that last message, but the site didn't permit even that much deviation from plain text.

I sighed audibly and sat on the toilet, waiting for Cerberus's reply.

I stared into the glowing screen as if devoured by it, alone in the bathroom stall.

But today, for the first time, Cerberus sent nothing back.

This had never happened before, not even once! It didn't matter what time of day I messaged him, early in the morning or late at night, he always replied right away!

Irritated, I refreshed the page again and again, furiously tapping the screen.

No change.

I rose from the toilet again and pulled up the pants I'd pushed down to my knees, then stuffed my phone back in my pocket.

And as I did, the toilet lid, as if compelled by an unseen force, suddenly closed, hitting me square in the butt.

. . .

RETURNING FROM THE bathroom, I saw that Michiyo and Taki had finished eating lunch but were still watching the torch relay.

Michiyo glanced up at me as I returned to my seat, then said, "Hey, you look a little pale. Everything all right?"

Taki looked up from the monitor and raised his eyebrows. "Yeah, are you okay?"

"Oh, I'm fine, just a little anemic," I replied—or rather, tried to reply, but for some reason my mouth wouldn't move properly, and the words came out garbled, like my tongue was in knots.

Taki and Michiyo stared at me, their eyes wide.

"Are you having trouble speaking? You know, when my grandpa had his stroke, it began with him being unable to say things right, too—be careful! If your arms and legs start tingling or you feel like you might throw up, tell us and we'll call an ambulance!"

Taki laughed. "Don't say that, it's bad luck! You shouldn't scare her—she's not the age to worry about strokes anyway." As he laughed, I saw a piece of carrot stuck in the gap between his two front teeth and recalled he'd been eating a veggie wrap for lunch.

But Michiyo shook her head, her expression grave.

"It happens to young people too. We ended up saving Grandpa's life, but he has memory loss now. If it happened today, we'd be worried he'd go Trinity."

She wrapped her lunch box back up in its cloth, looking at me hard as she continued.

"I'm serious, be careful. You remember that guy, that actor, what's his name? He had a brain hemorrhage or a blocked blood vessel in his head or something. Or that guitar player, remember him? He was one of those beta guys, you know, kinda wimpy—"

"Hey, now, that's enough!" Taki cut her off, still laughing. "You're the one who seems to be having memory problems here anyway!"

I felt truly sorry hearing about Michiyo's grandfather being unable to speak. Having my body and mind become useless due to a stroke really would be the end for me. The only saving grace was that he didn't end up as a Trinity, perhaps. My body shivered, and I tried to ignore the nausea rising up within me.

In any case, I decided it would be best to use my lunch break to go to the drugstore across the street.

WALKING OUTSIDE, I saw the sun had reached its zenith. Not a shadow to be found. Normally, I would consider it crazy to go outside this time of day, but I didn't feel like trying to make it through the afternoon without medicine. I slid on my long black gloves and opened my silver umbrella.

As I started to cross the street, I encountered a small demonstration.

A group of no more than thirty protesters holding signs and musical instruments marched up and down the sun-saturated sidewalk, following some middle-aged men and women holding a banner.

HELL NO, WE WON'T GLOW!
ALL THESE NUKES HAVE GOT TO GO!

A group of police, including some cars and motorbikes, hovered nearby—though many fewer than were at the Olympic torch relay.

There weren't just adults and children among the protestors, but older people as well.

These older people wore wide-brimmed hats and draped cold packs wrapped in towels around their necks. Mothers passing with their children would catch sight of them and quickly step into the road, dragging their children by the hand.

I, too, found myself leaving as much space as possible as I passed them by.

HELL NO, WE WON'T GLOW!
ALL THESE NUKES HAVE GOT TO GO!

The chants repeated as they marched.

Looking from afar, I wondered if the sun wouldn't do the old-timers in before the nukes had a chance to. I stifled my own nausea, standing there on the burning asphalt.

And besides, how did they propose we get rid of the nukes anyway?

Perhaps we could bury them deep beneath the surface of the earth in a vast underground facility like the Onkalo Spent Nuclear Fuel Repository in Finland.

Or perhaps we could encase it all in thick cement and throw it into the deepest part of the sea.

But the truth was, ridding the entire world of radioactive material was as difficult as ridding the entire world of stones, or of old people. And besides, no matter how deeply you buried it, surely someone would come along and try to dig it all back up. Just like now, with the accursed stones.

As I was thinking this, a middle-aged man wearing a bandana ran up to me and held out a handbill. It was a black-and-white xerox copy covered in tiny, seemingly handwritten characters. I took it before I quite knew what I was doing and instantly regretted it, but it was too late.

I looked around, but the garbage can next to the post box and the one in front of the nearby convenience store had both been sealed up as a counter terrorism measure.

I opened my bag to discreetly stuff the handbill inside and caught sight of a stone. It startled me.

It was the stone I'd tripped on coming into work. I'd purposely put it in my bag to throw it away but instead forgot it entirely.

I hurriedly covered the stone with the handbill and re-closed my bag as if sealing it up too.

Two children with their mothers were playing in front of the convenience store, laughing as they picked up stones and held them to their ears in imitation of old people.

Did you hear?
There's such a nice smell after a hydrogen bomb explodes!
It's the smell of ozone, you know!

I bought some headache medicine at the drugstore and opened it right next to the register. A dose was meant to be one pill, but I swallowed three in one gulp, washing it down with distilled water from my thermos. I started to walk out of the store, but just then my phone began vibrating in my pocket. I stopped to answer it, standing before rows and rows of shampoo bottles on shelves that stretched up to the ceiling.

All that showed on the screen was the number.

Filled with trepidation, I pushed the button to receive the call and brought the phone to my ear.

"Hello, excuse me for bothering you, but would this be Sensei's daughter?"

I heard a woman's voice in my ear.

"Sensei was so good to me over the years, teaching me how to make lace."

As she talked, I deduced that she must be a devoted student of the classes my mother used to teach at the antique store. *I remember meeting you back then as a young lady, and I could scarcely believe it when I learned that you'd grown up and now have a young lady of your own! Goodness, where does the time go?* She went on and on, speaking as any older person might to the daughter of a long-lost friend, but I couldn't for the life of me recall ever meeting her.

"I apologize for calling out of the blue like this. Mitsuko kindly provided me with your number."

The antique store lady.

Oh, right, the tax cheat—I almost said it aloud, but caught myself in time. All that came out was an inarticulate growl.

The woman gave no sign of noticing, though, and kept talking nonstop into my ear.

"I was going back and forth about whether to call you, but in these times, I couldn't help but think of your mother, how she might be doing. It would be so wonderful to hear she's doing all right, you know, it's just—"

The woman's affected voice and overly polite way of talking made it seem like she was never going to get to the point. She ended up trailing off, repeating "It's just—" a few times before going completely silent.

The unpleasantly cheerful company jingle blaring from the drugstore's sound system filled my ears, while my nose was assaulted by a mix of artificial fragrances from the shampoo bottles lined up before my eyes.

The woman, having seemingly resolved at last to cut to the chase, resumed speaking.

"So, well, I'm not sure quite how to put this, but I was just thinking, with all the things happening recently, I mean with these terrible terrorist incidents I've been hearing about, and now with the Opening Ceremony of the Olympics coming up and all these rumors . . ."

I was suddenly all ears.

"What I mean is, I don't want to imply that Sensei is one of those older people everyone talks about, I don't mean to imply that at all. After all, Sensei was able to create the most complex lace patterns so easily, whenever she felt like it . . . but still, it's just—"

It's just—

What did this woman want to tell me? Perhaps it was the shampoo smell, but my gorge was rising again.

It's just—

I heard the woman take an audible breath within the phone I was holding to my ear.

"It's just—Sensei's blog. I'd been reading it for a long time, but it seemed like she'd quit writing it. I would go there and never find a new update. I was quite worried, you understand. *Oh, I hope Sensei's all right,* I thought, so you can imagine how happy I was when I received a notification that the blog had been updated again after so long! I borrowed my husband's computer and went right away to see what Sensei had written, and I found that long, strange post . . . well, if it means that Sensei is feeling well again, that's wonderful, of course—it's just . . ."

I was at a total loss for words at this, and I took the phone from my ear. I tapped the screen, bringing up the browser. I scrolled through my bookmarks. Buried at the bottom of the list, there it was: *Lacework Diary.* I tapped the name. I could still faintly hear the woman's voice as she heedlessly continued speaking somewhere in the depths of my phone.

A small circle appeared in the white field on-screen as the page loaded. The time it took felt like an eternity.

The drugstore's air-conditioning was turned up so high it actually felt cold, but my fingers and forehead were still slick with sweat; I felt it running down the back of my neck, as well.

Pictures of lace appeared one by one as the page continued to load.

A lacework vest placed on light-blue construction paper for the photo.

A pineapple-patterned doily under an alarm clock.

And then—I felt my breath catch in my throat.

Sunday, July 16

All night I could hear the frogs in the nearby pond as they mated.

It was five a.m. The winds and thunder and rain had passed. It would be a clear dawn.

The men had their money out and were making wagers.

So what will it be, boy or girl?

A dollar on boy.

A dollar on girl . . .

It was that diary! The diary buried in Mother's laptop, that I—that *we*, my sister and I—thought we'd buried even deeper by dragging it to the trash can. The diary that should be long gone, deleted, banished . . .

The date on the post read `7/24/2020 12:00:00`—in other words, noon today.

I grew dizzy looking at all the zeros lined up in the time stamp.

A scheduled post.

That must be it: sometime in the past, quite a while ago in fact, Mother must have set this post to go up on this day at this time.

Why hadn't we thought of that?

Our fastidious mother had always set her posts to go up at the same time on the same day every week.

We were so mistaken to stop at just deleting the file from the computer.

I'd checked the desktop trash over and over, yet never thought to check the blog itself!

The woman's voice was still going on and on, faintly audible from the phone in my hand.

There were already several comments on the post.

Finger trembling, I tapped the screen.

What number crochet hook did you use to make the doily under the clock?

This seemed to be a comment meant for a different post.

I went on to the next one.

My mother (age 83) has lately been repeating a story very similar to the one written out here. She has dementia, so we're getting worried. I just stumbled onto this page after one of my regular Google searches. Thank you for your attention and for allowing me to post my comment.

And then the next one:

Forgive me for hijacking this thread, but my father-in-law has started repeating the same thing—we're very worried too. I saw what people were saying on Twitter so I came here to see for myself. I posted a question on Yahoo Answers as well and people replied that it was surely Trinity and I should take him to the hospital, but he's refusing to go.

And the next:

I'm wondering, is that doily woven from gold thread meant to be in the shape of the Gadget's core?

There were others after that, as well.

Gripped by terror, I hung up on the woman and closed the browser window.

My screen went dark.

But closing a browser window didn't make what it showed disappear from the world.

I knew I had to take down that blog.

I wondered if the password was the phone number from the old house too.

I took a series of deep breaths, and then, with a final exhale, summoned the resolve to confront my phone and its screen once more.

I went to Twitter and felt the blood drain from my body.

Trinity

Trinity

Trinity

There were screenshots from Mother's blog all over the site.

A message from a Trinity warning of another impending terrorist attack!

There were all sorts of theories and speculations flying around, attempting to tie Mother's post to the other incidents that had happened.

I staggered where I stood.

How could I possibly erase every mention, every screenshot, one by one?

It was only a matter of time before the identity of the blog's author was exposed, then the email addresses of her family, then their—our—address and phone number.

Would my sister be able to do something, as an IT person?

Maybe she could.

But can you really remove data from the internet once it's leaked—can you ever make it like it had never been?

Can we really make anything—information, radiation, stones—disappear from the world once it appears?

My phone began to vibrate in my hand.

A message from my sister.

Mother's gone.

13:00

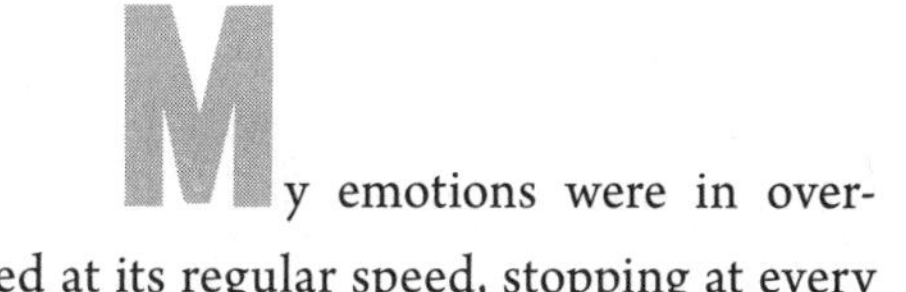

My emotions were in overdrive, but the train moved at its regular speed, stopping at every stop just like always. My sister's last message to me ended with her saying her phone was out of battery, and when I tried calling my daughter, it just rang and rang with no answer.

On the other hand, I was receiving countless notifications that Michiyo was calling me from the office. Even now, my phone was abuzz in my hand as she tried yet again.

I'd left the drugstore and, before I quite knew what I was doing, found myself on the train.

I'd shown up for work without fail for almost twenty years, and I didn't know myself what exactly I thought I was doing now. But I did know this was an emergency.

I have to answer Michiyo. But it occurred to me that Michiyo might have seen Mother's blog and that was why she was calling. As soon as I had the thought, my finger froze in fright, and I found myself unable to tap the screen to accept her call.

I knew what I had to do. I knew how hard it would be to find a new job at my age if I got fired. Would I be able to get by relying on my sister for support? The land where the old house had stood was now a vacant lot, but it hadn't sold yet. What would we do about the loan for the new condo? As these thoughts swirled around in my head, my phone stopped vibrating, as if giving up, exhausted.

I tried to soothe my unease by searching the internet. My fingers were still shaking, making it hard to tap the screen effectively, but I was able to go back to Mother's blog and scroll through more of the comments piling up on today's post.

It had become a gathering place for families who suspected their older relatives were going Trinity to post their concerns.

The rate of comments being added to the thread seemed to be accelerating now that screenshots were flying around the internet. There was plenty of anti-Trinity invective mixed in, *Terrorist!* and the like, and the number of comments kept swelling even as I watched.

People on Twitter were proposing theories linking the blog to Trinities like the Radium Princess and Saint Joachim's Valley.

This is a major warning from a new Trinity!

Beware the old people around you!

Predictions and suppositions about a possible terrorist attack on the Olympics Opening Ceremony were popping up all over the internet.

I heard Mansai Nomura doubled his bodyguards!

Yuriko Koike's coming to the ceremony in a bulletproof vehicle.

Don't forget to bring your iodine and Geiger counter if you go!

Trinity

Trinity

Trinity

My phone began to vibrate once more in my hand.

I didn't recognize the number.

Was this someone who saw Mother's blog?

Was my phone number already published somewhere on the internet?

I felt faint, my consciousness leaving me.

We must find Mother.

THE TRAIN STOPPED at the next station and two older women boarded, both with hair dyed jet black and wearing flashy clothes, one in a vivid red floral-print shirt, the other in polka dots. Their backpacks had thermoses and little Japanese flags stuffed in the outside pockets; they looked like they were heading out to an Opening Ceremony live-viewing party. They walked over to the seats reserved for older people, but then one stopped the other.

"No, we shouldn't!"

"You're right! It's too dangerous."

The two of them moved away from the seniors' seats, ending up sitting directly across from me.

They sat with both hands resting on their knees, as if showing they weren't carrying any guns or other weapons. A pose that said *No accursed stones here!*

Old people had taken to adopting this pose as a form of self-protection.

They tried to dress younger these days, too—trying to avoid being seen as "old people" as much as possible. They dyed their grey as soon as it appeared. They resisted the urge to stop short while walking in public. They tried to curb their tendency to ask the same question over and over. They refrained from asking directions even if they were lost. They kept their hands out of their pockets.

The most important thing was to seem cheerful, healthy, and young. This demanded the maximum attention and energy they could muster.

If this energy flagged, they might be outed as an old person, accused of being a Trinity and attacked—punched, surrounded, reported. It had become an issue of *personal responsibility.*

So, looking at the two women before me, though their manner and dress were vibrant and young, all I could see was how old they were.

Just as American soldiers supposedly saw every bearded Arab as another Osama bin Laden, I saw everyone older than me as "old."

The two women in front of me spoke to each other in exaggeratedly loud voices.

"Honestly, thanks to these Trinities, we can't even ride the train in peace!"

"I know—all we've done is quietly get older, yet we're the ones who end up paying for their actions!"

The woman in the polka-dotted shirt furrowed her brow. She spoke again, but this time in a hushed tone.

"But did you hear? This time it was arson . . ."

A SPRAWLING RESIDENTIAL neighborhood was passing by outside the train windows, creating complex patterns of shadow and light.

The train took a slow curve. The phone in my trembling hand vibrated again, this time showing a notification from a news site.

I tapped it and a video started playing automatically.

Re: was on fire.

Burned up, literally.

The apartment building where Re: had lived with her grandmother, the Radium Princess, had been set ablaze. The Radium Princess herself was still under investigation and in police custody, so she hadn't been at home. But Re:, who'd been allowed to leave, and an older couple who'd lived in the neighboring apartment sustained severe injuries. The couple eventually died, but Re: survived, though her entire body had been burned.

Fortunately, the other people who'd been living in the building had already moved out due to its impending demolition.

The fire spread fast through the old wooden building, wrapping it in a column of flame.

Watching it on my phone's screen, the fire gave off so much light—bigger, brighter, and more brilliant than even the Olympic torch's sacred flame.

Fire trucks pulled up, but their streams of water were no match for the fire's power.

The roof collapsed, sending up even more flames.

The collapse revealed a huge bodhi tree standing behind the building and an orderly row of just-constructed homes.

I kept watching the video.

Without that building, would the land it stood on finally be incorporated into the general gentrification sweeping the neighborhood? You might say the old couple who died saved everyone the trouble of arranging their cremation. Would a brand-new apartment building be constructed in its stead?

It looked likely it was arson, but there were plenty who'd thank the arsonist, it seemed.

Thank them for disposing of two old people, and for visiting fiery punishment upon the terrorist collaborator Re:.

Re: seemed likely to survive. Bathed in flames, her skin was surely a mass of keloid scars—but still, she'd live on. Perhaps for years to come. This string of incidents—like the Olympics, like the World's Fair, like everything—would slide into the past, until there was no one left to remember them. But for now Re: would live, her skin, exposed, telling its story.

I opened Re:'s blog.

Updates had stopped a few days before. I looked again at her self-portrait. She looked out from the photo like always, dressed in her star-patterned puff-sleeved blouse and flared black miniskirt, that neon-pink hairband in her hair. I noticed that a short self-introduction had been added beneath.

This is me, Re:

"'*Wir sind gewohnt dass die Menschen verhöhnen was sie nicht verstehen*—We are used to see that Man mocks what he never comprehends.' Goethe is always pithy."

Sherlock Holmes said that.

Just as I thought—still crazy! I tried to tell myself this, but I couldn't quite do it. I grew frightened, tapping furiously on the screen to blow Re:'s photo up as big as I could.

Her silver paintings appeared in my head.

Those flowers that remained, no matter how much paint was slathered over them.

Those flowers that would never disappear, even as they became invisible.

The two old women sitting before me on the train continued their conversation.

"It's so scary, isn't it?"

"But isn't it even worse to live too long and go Trinity?"

"That's true. I can't stand the thought of living so long I become a burden on others."

"If that ever happens to me, I'd rather die."

"Me too. And quickly!'

My hands were soaked in sweat.

"If I ever become a burden, that'll be it for me."

To avoid future bother *down below,* many women permanently remove the hair on their inner thighs and genitals.

So, what should be done to avoid the *future bother* of going Trinity?

It was getting harder and harder to breathe.

Her existence itself is a problem. Die! Make amends by dying!

But Re: hadn't died.

I FINALLY REACHED my station and got off the train; as I exited through the turnstile, I saw that the bands were just getting ready for their performances. The symphonic band from my daughter's school was walking out onstage, assembling themselves beneath the garish pink lights hung around the tent set up for shade. Folding chairs formed a semicircle in the stage's center.

The student musicians were all wearing T-shirts bearing the familiar Olympic blue-and-white-checked pattern on top and their regular school uniform skirts and pants on bottom. There were several of my daughter's classmates among them, and I recognized many faces in the group. I worked my way to the middle of the crowd so as to blend in.

The trumpets and trombones began to play.

The sun beat down. I moved the umbrella in my hand back and forth to help clear space as I proceeded upstream through the crowd.

Where on Earth did my mother go?

Old people wandered off. A care worker once told me that the phrase *wander off* was no longer used, as it wasn't considered accurate.

"They're not all wandering around with no clear destination, after all," she explained. "They're usually trying to get somewhere specific—they just tend to get lost along the way."

A man holding a beer can was using the towel around his neck to dab at the sweat streaming from his forehead.

A woman in a wide-brimmed hat was standing behind a video camera resting on a tripod.

The air was filled with the mingled odors of hot air, sweat, and sunblock.

There was a burst of applause.

A fanfare sounded.

I continued through the crowd as if fleeing its sound.

I finally broke through the far side of the crowd and into the train station roundabout. A small bus from a nursing home was parked there.

Someone had defaced it, writing in huge black spray-painted letters:

THE TERRORISTS HAVE ARRIVED!

My heart stopped.

SUNSET

Over everything—up through the wreckage of the city, in gutters, along the riverbanks, tangled among tiles and tin roofing, climbing on charred tree trunks—was a blanket of fresh, vivid, lush, optimistic green; the verdancy rose even from the foundations of ruined houses. Weeds already hid the ashes, and wild flowers were in bloom among the city's bones. The bomb had not only left the underground organs of plants intact; it had stimulated them. Everywhere were bluets and Spanish bayonets, goosefoot, morning glories and day lilies, the hairy-fruited bean, purslane and clotbur and sesame and panic grass and feverfew. Especially in a circle at the center, sickle senna grew in extraordinary regeneration, not only standing among the charred remnants of the same plant but pushing up in new places, among bricks and through cracks in the asphalt. It actually seemed as if a load of sickle-senna seed had been dropped along with the bomb.

—John Hersey, *Hiroshima* (1946)

14:00

The cream-colored curtains around the beds in the quiet hospital room were all drawn, the only illumination in the room the light from the television. I'd come running in through the door, panting. The bed nearest the window and furthest from the door, where Mother should have been, was the only one with its curtain pulled back, exposing its emptiness.

I pulled out my phone with one black-gloved hand, the other still holding my umbrella, as I stood with my legs shoulder-width apart facing the empty bed. Sweat streamed down my face with no sign of stopping despite the air-conditioning. Droplets slid from my forehead down my cheeks, then fell to the linoleum floor.

My daughter was sitting on a folding chair beside the bed, her sneakers up on the bedframe, staring up at the torch relay on the television with her mouth half-open. The rolling table next to the bed had my sister's iPad set up on it; a muted video was playing soundlessly on its screen. White lettering running down the side of the image read:

Beautiful Moment, Do Not Pass Away!: Seventeen Days in Munich
An Olympic Channel Special Presentation

Vivid color footage of men running as fast as they could was playing in extreme slow motion. Their cheeks, arms, and legs cut through the air, their flesh distorting: a single moment stretching into endlessness.

It reminded me of my life now, each moment tortured into an eternity.

Beautiful Moment, Do Not Pass Away!

It was a quote from Goethe's *Faust,* appropriated for the Japanese title of the documentary *Visions of Eight.*

I whispered the phrase to myself—or tried to, but again, my tongue disobeyed, and it came out as a garbled jumble.

The Munich Olympics.

I remembered Sawada-san bringing it up, back when I was at her house in Setagaya.

"It happened at the Munich Olympics, too, you know. A terrorist attack."

She said this while stroking her lavender-tinted hair, watching me loosening a nut beneath her sink with a hexagonal wrench.

"I just compared this neighborhood to Palestine, but I bet someone your age doesn't have much of an idea what 'Palestine' means—you weren't even born during the Munich Olympics, were you?"

And she was right, I was born well after they were held.

Beautiful Moment, Do Not Pass Away!

The men were still running full tilt through their eternal moment.

According to Sawada-san, Palestinian terrorists from a group called Black September kidnapped a group of Israeli athletes during the Munich Olympics. The whole world watched the events unfold live on their televisions. In the end, the attempt to rescue the hostages failed, and almost everyone—terrorists and athletes alike—was killed.

"It was really something. After that, the games themselves, truth be told, seemed almost boring in comparison.

"The Olympics may not have even been over before Israel began their strikes on Palestine. The Israeli army firebombed them from the air. The vengeance didn't stop at killing terrorists—they decimated their homeland, killing so many who just happened to live there.

"I remember having arguments every night with my husband over Palestine."

Sawada-san filled a teacup with water from the faucet where I'd just changed the filter and brought it to her Buddhist altar. In lieu of striking a match, she flicked a switch to "light" the LED candle.

"It was a dangerous time. So, it's really unsettling to see old people picking up stones and walking around with them these days."

The men had finally stopped running in slow motion. They were replaced by images of a man blowing an enormous horn and a woman in a folkloric costume ringing something that looked like a cowbell. No dead terrorists or hostages in sight.

Finally, my daughter noticed my arrival, turning her head toward me while leaning back in the folding chair.

"That was pretty quick, Mom."

Her feet still on the bedframe, she opened her mouth wide in a yawn.

My daughter's nonchalance sparked a rage that rose up from the pit of my stomach.

How can you be so calm, not bothering to answer the phone when I call? Your grandmother is missing!

My long black gloves, soaked in sweat, started to feel cold and clammy where they stuck to my skin.

But my daughter, indifferent to my upset, rocked her chair back and forth while adding, "Grandma has my phone anyway, you know. Though it's not like she knows how to use it."

And indeed, my daughter was using her right hand to pick at her lace vest as if she didn't know what else to do with it. The black phone she always carried, with its omnipresent DEATH BE NOT PROUD sticker, was nowhere to be seen.

An inarticulate moan escaped my lips.

I felt faint.

My mother ran away and took a smartphone with her?

What is going on?

In other words, it wasn't like she'd wandered off without her purse. If she had a smartphone, she could ride the train, take a taxi, buy whatever she felt like—a butcher knife, some gasoline . . .

And then, right as I was starting to run half-panicked to grab my daughter by the shoulders, it happened: my legs tangled together beneath me as if someone had tied them together. My umbrella struck the rolling table. The bag on my shoulder flew up into space, its contents falling to the ground. The hospital room resounded with the clatter of my things scattering across the linoleum. I found myself falling to the ground to join them.

"Mom? Are you okay?"

My daughter finally took her shoes off the bedframe, leaping to her feet.

I tried to signal that I was fine as I used my newly bent umbrella as a makeshift crutch to help raise myself off the ground. I began crawling around, gathering the things that had fallen out of my bag.

On the other side of the drawn curtains, all remained silent.

The color of the light from the television screen was the only thing that changed.

Looking up at it, I saw that the torch relay was still going on.

A young girl was running alone, surrounded on both sides by tall buildings.

She looked to be around eleven years old, maybe twelve. She was dressed in a white tank top and neon-pink leggings, and her hair was pulled up into two ponytails. She carried the silver torch in her right hand. This girl running beneath fire was sweating, her bangs sticking wetly to her cheeks and forehead.

White smoke trailed after her, wafting slowly upward in her wake as the roar of the cheering crowd greeted her.

Police trailed her as well, a profusion of cars and motorbikes and officers trotting along on foot.

Looking at this girl, I thought of that old woman who'd lived with Re:, the Radium Princess.

I'd read that even this old terrorist had once aspired to be a girl running with the Olympic torch.

Sad! A Tragic End for a Girl Who Had Been Denied Her Chance to Run in the Torch Relay for the Cancelled 1940 Tokyo Olympics!

This was the headline slapped on the story as it ran on an aggregator site.

That old lady had, of course, been a little girl once.

A little girl looking forward to the Olympics that were going to finally arrive in her country, her heart beating fast at the thought of carrying the torch's sacred fire, her entire being filled with hopes and dreams, with the thought that she could grow up to become anything she wished.

My daughter was down on her knees beside me, helping me gather up everything that had scattered across the floor.

Comparing the young girl on the television with my daughter beside me, I slid my hand into my bag.

My fingers touched something hard and cold.

The stone.

The stone I'd tripped over this morning, that I'd buried in the very bottom of my bag and meant to throw away—that stone.

That stone that should have been long gone by now, forgotten.

My vision grew hazy.

The little girl the old woman had once been had been inspired by photos she'd seen in her girls' magazines of the Berlin Olympics.

The Nazi Olympics, led by Adolf Hitler.

In Greece, at the ruins of the Temple of Olympia, eleven virgins used mirrors to gather the light of the sun.

The sun's light, its fire, the same that Prometheus stole to give to humanity.

A sacred fire, reborn.

This is the fire borne by the Olympic torch.

As my fingers touched the stone, I heard a voice speak, faintly.

Sacred fire passed from hand to hand. This was the world's first Olympic torch relay.

It ran from Olympia, Greece, to Berlin, Germany.

It took twelve days and 3,308 runners.

The voice spoke directly through my body, through my head. It was a voice that was not a voice.

I shivered in fear and surprise.

And at the same time, I found myself drawn to it, to this stone I couldn't seem to get rid of, to this voice that was not a voice.

I curled my body so my ear would be closer to the stone.

As I did, a landscape appeared in my head—a small village, swept up in anticipation of the Berlin Olympics.

A large crowd had gathered, looking up.

A ladder was set against the stone wall of a red-roofed building.

The five rings of the Olympic emblem had been carved into the wall.

And beneath them, the year: 1936.

As the last ring was completed, a cry went up from the crowd.

The people gathered at the base of the ladder began to talk excitedly among themselves.

They spoke in German. But I nonetheless found myself able to understand every word.

A man, still staring up at the rings, muttered his complaint.

Why is the sacred fire passing through Teplitz when it could just as easily pass through Karlovy Vary?

A woman standing next to him agreed.

It's the Olympics—I wanted to be able to see the torch pass! A glimpse, at least!

A different man cut in, shouting.

I wanted to see those snappy Wehrmacht soldiers too!

The rumor was that Berlin was prosperous and rich.

The sacred fire's route started in Prague at 1:00 a.m. on July 31, then passed through Straskov at 4:30, Terezín at 6:15, and finally through Teplitz at 9:00. Even Teplitz, the nearest city to where this crowd had gathered, was still a hundred kilometers away.

This was Sankt Joachimsthal—Saint Joachim's Valley.

On the *Silberstraße,* which ran straight through town to the church on the hill.

The ladder was removed from the stone wall.

The newly carved Olympic emblem was all that remained.

But that was okay.

For I knew.

The sacred fire of the Berlin Olympics may not have reached this place, but soon enough the Nazi army would. Two years after the Olympics, the German army, as if tracing the torch's path in reverse, would invade. The torch may have passed this place by on its way to Nazi Germany, but eventually Nazi Germany would come to it, riding in tanks manufactured by the same company that made the torch itself, engulfing all in its path in flame.

"Mom?

"Mom, are you all right?"

I came to and saw my daughter peering into my face.

Back to my senses, I hurriedly released the stone from my grasp.

My daughter stood before me, her brows knit, staring at me.

"Your color isn't very good . . ."

She spoke with concern, but I just shook my head and waved her away with both hands.

My daughter tended to act, not just with Mother but with me as well, as if we were elderly and sick. But I was still young, I'd never had a major illness in my life, I was healthier than almost anyone when it came to what I put in my body, the water I drank, the food I ate . . .

Looking back up at the television, the young girl was still running, her pigtails dancing in the breeze.

I slyly reached back in the bag, grabbing the stone again without my daughter noticing.

The sacred fire, it was supposed to come here . . .

As I held the stone in my bag, the voice returned, flowing up from where my fingertips touched it.

. . . here, this time in Tokyo!

The 1940 Tokyo Olympics. Set to coincide with the celebrations for the 2,600th anniversary of the founding of Japan.

A grand torch relay was planned: Olympia to Athens, then to Istanbul, Ankara, Tehran, Kabul, Peshawar, Delhi, Kolkata, Hanoi, Guangdong, Tianjin, Seoul, Busan . . . the sacred fire was to be borne by men on foot and on horseback, its light crossing Eurasia eastward hand to hand until it reached the Land of the Rising Sun.

Would the Latin phrase *ex oriente lux*—light comes from the East—end up changing to *ex occidente lux*—light comes from the West?

But in the end, the sacred fire never made it here—its light never reached Tokyo.

The Olympics were never held.

I gently removed my fingers from the stone. It slid slowly to the bottom of my bag.

Not content to retrace the route of the never-completed torch relay across Asia, Imperial Japan also struck east, all the way to the U.S., to Hawaii, using bombers in lieu of horses, engulfing all in its path in flame.

That little girl grew older, and eventually was no longer a little girl at all. Youth, like so many things, is fleeting.

"Mom?

"Mom!"

My daughter was looking hard at me.

I snatched the thermos she was offering me and poured distilled water down my throat. Liquid dribbled from the corners of my mouth, but it seemed too much of a bother to wipe it away.

"Mom, I think you should go to the hospital."

My daughter said this to me in all sincerity—but weren't we already in a hospital?

I crawled over to a chair and used it to pull myself up, finally managing to sit up in it.

Scenes from the Munich Olympics continued even now to play on the iPad set up on the rolling table. Wrestlers cried silently in defeat as they lay prone or curled on their sides in the ring.

My daughter just looked at me, shaking her head.

"Mom."

She remained standing, looking down at me.

Was she trying to intimidate me?

I sat frozen, looking sheepishly back up at her.

Had my sister told her something before I got here?

Had she read her grandmother's blog post?

She might know—she could very well know everything!

Trinity

Trinity

Trinity

Sweat streamed down my forehead, down my sides.

Or maybe, just maybe, she had something completely different to tell me! Maybe she has a new boyfriend! I tried to tell myself jokes, but I couldn't make myself laugh.

My daughter muttered under her breath, as if spitting the words out.

"Mom, you don't see . . ."

There seemed to be no movement or life behind the curtains in the other beds. But perhaps there really were people there—they were just motionless with suspense, hanging on our every word. Or perhaps they were waiting for us to leave so they could scan the room with Geiger counters.

"You don't even *try* to see what's really going on with me!"

My daughter picked the iPad up and began touching the screen, fiddling with something.

I couldn't figure out what she might be referring to.

It seemed laughable—I didn't even *try* to see? Really?

I stared at my daughter's face as she looked down at the iPad.

What more was I supposed to see—what more *could* I see of this girl who'd emerged from my own body?

From the moment I emerged from my mother's body, I already had within me the egg in my ovaries that would become my daughter, along with the womb to nourish her. I'd cared for this presence within me for over a quarter century until it became my daughter, and looked after her for over a decade after that—what had I been paying attention to all these years if not her?

"What a joke."

My daughter passed me the iPad by throwing it onto the empty bed in front of me. Then she wordlessly grabbed her bag and headed out the door without a second look.

I tried to stop myself, but a moan escaped my lips.

I watched as my daughter disappeared down the hall.

It was the middle of summer, but she still dressed head-to-toe in black, her ratty black bag containing God knows what slung on her back; it bore a patch with that omnipresent DEATH BE NOT PROUD slogan on it. But for a brief moment, a shaft of sunlight illuminated her, and I saw her so clearly—that white lace vest; her jet-black, too-short hair that stuck up all over; the tears shining in her eyes—and then, just as suddenly, she was gone.

I sat speechless in my chair, then looked down at where she'd thrown the iPad.

Its screen showed a street map.

A pulsing ball of pale blue light was moving slowly up the map.

It took me some time to realize what that ball of pale light signified. But when I did, my eyes almost popped out of my head.

A miracle.

A technological miracle!

The map was showing Mother carrying my daughter's phone. The GPS was still on, so it was using that to track her movements. Wherever that pale glow went, that's where my mother would be.

It seemed to be moving toward the center of Tokyo.

The dense green of the Meiji Shrine filled the center of the map, surrounded by a cloud of train station names.

Staring at them, it came to me where she must be heading.

The Japan National Stadium—now known as the Olympic Stadium.

She was heading for the Opening Ceremony!

15:00

The taxi inched along, then stopped. I was sitting in the back seat, staring at the ball of light pulsing on the screen of the iPad resting on my knees. The taxi was one of the cramped older models, not the roomier kind more prevalent now, and there was a screen mounted on the back of the seat in front of me soundlessly showing ads for employment agencies.

The concert in front of the station seemed to have just ended. A wave of people leaving the station was choking the roadway, slowing traffic to a stop-and-start crawl.

The driver raised a white-gloved hand to his mouth and coughed.

"You know, what with the torch relay and the Olympics and the terrorism precautions, the roads are pretty much always like this these days."

Blue and pink Olympic mascots hung from his rearview mirror along with the usual good-luck charms.

The driver glanced at me via the mirror.

"You want to go to the stadium—I take it you're attending the Opening Ceremony? Lucky . . .

"My wife and daughter, they're going to a park for one of those, whattaya call 'em, 'viewing parties'—you know, where they show a live feed on a big screen somewhere? They're going all that way just for that. Really looking forward to it, even.

"Things have gotten really crazy for me, too, because of the Olympics . . . but nothing's more important than *hos-pi-tal-i-ty,* right?"

Sitting in the backseat, my brow furrowed in concentration and worry, I found it too much of a bother to even nod along with this monologue.

The meter kept silently ticking up and up.

¥810

¥890

¥970

Looking out the taxi window, I saw people passing by, sweating in the heat, towels wrapped around their necks or around their heads. I recognized some of my daughter's classmates as they walked by in the blinding sunlight. The girls were holding ice treats from the convenience store in their hands, their sun-kissed cheeks glowing as they chatted and messed around. I could see the bra straps of one through her white T-shirt. Laughing, the girls passed by my stationary taxi, completely unaware that I was watching from inside.

Remembering my own daughter, the breath caught in my throat.

What was she telling me to see?

I was so cold—the taxi's air-conditioning was turned up too high. My tingling hands wouldn't stop shaking.

Irritated, I turned off the video playing in front of my face, striking the button on the monitor as if hitting it.

The taxi began to move again, though slowly.

We were passing by the roundabout beside the station. The neon-pink lights hung around the stage dazzled my eyes.

I brought the phone in my hand up to my face. An unseen force unlocked the screen. I forced my trembling hands to tap it, navigating to the Trinity site.

Still no answer from Cerberus.

I decided to write him a message anyway.

<< I want to do it so bad with you, Cerberus. Right now

<< I want you so bad that if I knew where you were, I'd gladly show up on your doorstep and knock on your door, panty-less and ready

I just want you to hear me.

I just want you to save me.

I continued typing, though my fingers wouldn't stop trembling.

They would slip and I'd make a typo, but I didn't care. I'd just continue.

`<< Cerberus, I want to meet you`

`<< I want to touch the real you, I want to put the real you inside me`

`<< I want to see you`

I was calling out to him. Again and again, calling out to him.

I noticed that as I touched my phone, my trembling fingers were actually making a shape. A cross.

Cross after cross as I tapped the screen.

Like a prayer.

Cerberus, please respond!

I don't care what kind of perverted things you might want to do with me!

In the name of the Father, the Son, and the Holy Ghost. Amen.

The pulsing ball of light continued its steady progress up the map on the iPad.

AFTER TAKING A variety of detours and alternate routes, we finally reached the Tokyo Metropolitan Expressway.

The taxi accelerated, unleashed at last. We passed through the electronic toll gate and merged into traffic. Grey and brown buildings lined both sides of the expressway.

As we moved through this new landscape as if through the bottom of a valley, I remembered seeing on TV that the expressway had been built in anticipation of the 1964 Tokyo Olympics. Which meant that at the same time my mother and father were buying their land and building their house, ground was being broken and bridges were being built so that the airport and Tokyo's downtown could be connected directly. Bars and clubs considered too "immoral" for the Olympics disappeared, swept from the streets as part of the general cleanup. There wasn't a speck of litter to be found by the time Self-Defense Force jets were tracing five perfect rings in the spotless blue sky.

That was when my mother first planted the fig tree in the yard. She'd planted it with her own two hands, that tree that bore the fruit she'd later reach for, causing her to slip, breaking her leg. All those bars changed their names, called themselves "diners" and started serving snacks, while that tree grew year after year until it was tall and covered in fruit. Perhaps if different decisions had been made, the present would have been different, a separate now from the one in which we found ourselves.

A single white thread, woven into a pattern.

A single white thread of lace yarn that passed through the golden crochet hooks held in my mother's hands, twisting, coiling, knotting, looping.

Each tiny loop building on the next, until a grand pattern emerged.

1
2
3
4
5

Her lips moved in concert with the hooks.

They were painted a beautiful red.

My mother was young, beautiful.

Her long eyelashes fluttered.

Her dark eyes fixed me with their gaze.

I caught my breath, looking at her.

My mother, looking straight at me, reached for a shiny black stone.

A shiny black stone that normally rested atop the end table next to the sofa.

My mother closed her fingers around it, then raised it to her ear.

She closed her eyes. She listened.

I was so young then. I asked her:

Can you hear it?

My mother, her eyes shut tight, remained silent.

I held my breath, waiting.

My mother slowly opened her eyes.

I hear it.

And then she picked up her golden hooks and continued weaving the rest of the yarn.

1

2

3

4

5

She wove the voice of the stone into the lace.

The same way scenes from history are woven into tapestries.

It's all I know how to do, after all.

And besides, before you two were born, I had a lot of time on my hands.

And so, by the time we were born, every surface in the house where my sister and I grew up was covered in my mother's lace. When my sister was just starting to walk, she liked to suck on her thumb and then use the tiny wet appendage to trace its patterns. She would giggle and shriek as she did.

It's like she can read the story woven into the pattern!

Watching, I would laugh as well.

I hope one day I can start to hear those stories too.

I extended my hand toward the stone. My fingertips touched its shining black surface.

My mother heard the stone's voice.

She'd known how to do it all along—it wasn't a matter of forgetting.

Though it seemed that most Trinities started to remember how to hear the stone's voice when they started to forget everything else.

My father loved stones, and he loved my mother as she listened to them.

My father always wore the watch she'd given him—I don't think he ever took it off.

He would call us over, my sister and me.

Look, he'd say.

This watch was painted with radium paint, in America, by the company Westclox. This is a special, rare watch, made back when they used radium paint to make clock faces glow in the dark!

My mother had found the watch in her friend Mitsuko's antique shop, and it was unclear whether she realized its glow came from the radium paint's high level of radioactivity.

My father would slowly cup his palm over the watch.

Beneath the shadow, its face would glow fluorescent green.

My sister and I would cry out, our eyes wide.

Sometimes Mother would join in too: *Wow!*

We would all gather around, shading the watch's face to see its faint light illuminate the darkness we created.

My father would pull out the glass case containing his rock specimens and take out a black, shiny stone.

This is uranite. Pitchblende.

It contains radium.

He would hold out his palm.

There it would be: the black, black stone.

But no matter how hard we stared, that's all it remained: a black stone.

No fluorescent green, no glow.

Seeing my lips tighten in disappointment, my father would laugh.

Only about 0.0001% of this rock is radium!

There's so little, it's not even visible to the naked eye.

But if you gather tons and tons of it...

My father would close his hand over the stone.

He would blow on it.

And then he would open his hand again.

There, in place of the stone, would lay the watch.

If you gather up enough of these tiny traces, you'll eventually get enough to see, even to glow!

And indeed, there in my father's hand, the watch would glow.

To think such a beautiful green light was buried deep in that black stone.

It was only much later that I learned why they no longer make watches using this marvelous glowing radium paint.

The factory girls who painted the faces of these watches would lick their fine-tipped brushes, and one by one, they succumbed to radiation poisoning and died. They became anemic, their bones so brittle their jaws would break; they say that radiation can be detected even now rising up from their graves.

The windowsill was full of vases and glassware that shone in the sunlight so fluorescent green they were hard to look at directly. Beyond them grew the young fig tree, verdant and lively if not yet fruit-bearing, its leaves unfurling to catch the light of the sun.

OUR FATHER'S MOTHER—our grandmother—was the only one to find our mother's habits unsettling.

As she checked the envelopes our father would give her again and again to make sure the money was still in them, she'd take us aside before she left.

Your mother seems to love listening to that thing's *voice. It's not right. You know how many people died thanks to* that thing?

Then she would fish out a match and light yet another cigarette, crossing herself discreetly as she did.

They say her rich parents died young—but do we know for sure it was just a coincidence? I wonder . . .

White smoke would stream out from the gap between her two protruding front teeth.

Oh Lord, deliver us from evil. Amen.

You lot may be wise to watch yourselves, too, you know.

Our grandmother would warn us.

She passed away the same year I entered elementary school.

The miracle she prayed for never came.

MY SISTER AND I spent her funeral imitating her, crossing ourselves and pretending to blow smoke between our teeth before dissolving into giggles.

In the parking lot outside the crematorium, we picked up rocks and held them to our ears.

Can you hear it?

My sister and I stared into each other's eyes.

I hear it.

I lied.

No matter how hard I tried, I could never hear a thing.

Smoke rose in a thin white thread from the crematorium's smokestack.

Our grandmother's flesh was burning up, disappearing.

I realized now that my sister may not have been pretending back then—she may very well have been able to hear the stone's voice.

16:30

The LCD screen on the taxi's GPS showed our progress as an arrow moving along a white line that wound its way through the map. Numbers at the top right showed the time to be four-thirty p.m.

I unscrewed the top of my thermos with shaking hands and poured distilled water down my throat. It leaked from the corners of my mouth to run down my chin and neck and even dribble onto my knees.

The ball of faint blue light on the screen of the iPad in my lap had come to a stop at the stadium, its slow pulse now its only movement. I glanced at the bag I'd set down next to me and caught sight of the black-and-white handbill I'd stuffed in it—the one

I was unable to throw away in front of the drugstore earlier. I finally read the tiny handwritten characters crowding its surface.

> ***Now is the time we must listen to what the stones are telling us!***
>
> ***We must, with our own two hands, recover our ability to hear them!***
>
> ***There was once a time when everyone heard the voice of the stones.***
>
> ***But now we live in a world ruled by utilitarianism, and we've forgotten what we once knew.***
>
> ***The time has come to reawaken these ancient memories!***
>
> ***From the sacred land of Kakadu, Australia, a message was sent from time immemorial—a terrible force unleashed upon the world, excavated from the ground—for it was uranium ore from Kakadu that fueled the Fukushima Dai-ichi Nuclear Power Plant!***

The taxi entered a long tunnel.

Newly frightened, I stuffed the handbill back down into the bottom of my bag.

I shook my head as I did, as if refusing the world around me.

It's not true, it can't be true—there must be some mistake!

I must find Mother!

The tunnel curved gently, cutting off the sun and replacing it with rows of LED lights that slid by the taxi windows at regular intervals. I remembered that this tunnel had been used in an old science fiction movie as the landscape of the future, though even that future was now part of the past.

MY SISTER BEGAN her avoidance of our mother the spring she began attending elementary school.

It started with her stuffing all the lace clothing Mother had made for her into a big black garbage bag and throwing it away.

"I can't wear this stuff—no one wears lace anymore!"

This was the explanation my sister spit out when Mother asked why she'd thrown it away, and then she shut herself into her room, not even emerging to eat dinner.

Mother thought she must have been bullied at school.

I took it upon myself the next today to see if that was true and snuck down the stairs to peek into her classroom during lunch break. I saw her sitting apart from a group of girls, her chin resting on her hands. The room was dimly illuminated by overhead fluorescent tubes.

My sister wasn't crying. She hadn't been hit. No one was yelling at her. She wasn't bleeding. Her gym clothes hadn't been ripped up.

My sister was fine.

Just fine.

There was no bullying here.

I chose to believe in the truth of the visible.

The sky was white where I could see it through the classroom windows. It was raining.

The raindrops left tracks where they slid down the glass.

My sister refused to speak to our mother the next day and the day after that, and she refused to wear the lace clothing Mother made for her. Though almost none of it was left anyway.

Late at night, I would lay on the top bunk of our bed staring at the knots in the wood grain of the ceiling. I would whisper to my sister as she tossed and turned on the bottom bunk beneath me.

"Can you hear it?"

I waited for her answer. I strained my ears for it.

But it never came.

The rain continued to fall outside the window.

The still-young fig tree just visible in the shadowy yard unfurled its leaves to catch the raindrops as they fell.

An accident had occurred at the Chernobyl Nuclear Power Plant in the Soviet Union.

This thing called radiation, invisible to the naked eye, was falling along with the rain.

On the television, they said countries all across Europe were recording high levels of it in their environment.

They found it even in their milk.

The Soviet Union tried to cover up the extent of the damage, but it had reached a point where that would no longer work.

Radiation.

It terrified me.

When it rained down on you, at first nothing would happen, but then you would lose your hair, you would bleed and be unable to stop, your skin would split and slough off.

Footage showing the broken reactor tower played on television; it had been taken by a Soviet cameraman who'd ridden in a helicopter over the power plant. The footage would occasionally turn bright white, obliterating the image, before going back to normal again. This wasn't a technical problem with the camera, they said, but rather bursts of radiation from the plant registering on the film. I learned later that the cameraman himself died soon after taking the footage.

I also heard rumors that exposure to radiation would make you unable to have children.

Or, if you did, the children would be stillborn or plagued by birth defects.

But I also heard that a good defense against radiation was vodka.

I heard that fermented foods like miso and natto were good, too. I heard that people who'd been poisoned by radiation had eaten miso soup and regained their health.

I sat there, square in the middle of the living room, and devoured the images playing across the cathode-ray tubes of the television, shivering in fear.

The rain continued day after day.

When I walked home from school, I'd grow frightened if water splashed up on my ankles and would hurry home to towel them dry right away. Though they said that no matter how hard you wiped, the radioactive particles would stay in your body, never to leave.

I would nonetheless scrub myself hard with soap in the bath too.

Sunday came but the rain didn't stop.

First thing in the morning, I started watching tabloid news shows on the television.

I learned about a popular "radiation rice bowl" being sold that featured strips of dried kombu seaweed, thick wakame, and natto.

Our father was up in his study on the second floor, leaving our mother, having finished cleaning up after breakfast, free to sit on the deep-green velvet sofa and make lace. The piece she was working on was spread out over her knees; it looked big enough to be on its way to becoming a tablecloth.

That morning my sister had slept late and was now standing in the kitchen chewing on a bread stick. She was watching the tabloid news out of the corner of her eye until finally, clucking her tongue impatiently, she walked over and snatched the remote control from my hand and changed the channel.

To a shopping network. A middle-aged man and woman were extolling the healing powers of a magnetic necklace. *And if you order one now, you'll receive a second one free!*

Angry, I turned to my sister.

"I was watching that!"

Ignoring me, my sister went to the refrigerator, took out a carton of milk, and poured herself a glass. The carton was decorated with cartoon cows dancing in a farmyard, making me think that perhaps they'd been touched by radiation as well.

"Hey, c'mon, I said I was watching that!"

I kept complaining but my sister kept ignoring me, her gaze fixed on our mother as if I wasn't even there. Our mother had the shiny black stone in her hand and was holding it to her ear. Lace flowed in waves over her knees.

My sister's face contorted in anger.

It was as if she'd been confronted by something deeply obscene.

"Stop that!"

Her voice was low, almost a growl.

"Stop 'listening to the stone,' it creeps me out—just stop it!"

Mother, startled, raised her eyes.

She slowly took the stone from her ear.

At nearly the same moment, my sister threw the glass of milk in her hand across the room.

The glass hit the brushed-plaster wall beside the sofa and shattered.

The shiny black rock slipped from my mother's fingertips.

Milk flew everywhere, leaving a white stain on the framed picture of the sun rising over farmland.

My sister's face was white too.

I sat there watching, speechless.

Hearing the commotion, our father came down from the second floor.

My sister, still rooted to the spot, began to sob convulsively.

Mother picked up the black stone and put it in her pocket, then industriously began cleaning up the glass on the floor. The piece of lace she'd been working on was draped over the sofa where she'd set it aside, almost reaching the ground.

I did as she told me and got a dishcloth from the kitchen to begin wiping up the spilled milk. Our father intervened and replaced me.

"I don't want you to cut yourself on the glass."

And so, the two of us, my sister and I, watched as our parents cleaned up milk and glass.

Even after they were all done and everything was tidy again, as if nothing had happened at all, my sister continued to sob.

Father sidled up to her and said, softly, "What do you think, can everything go back the way it was?"

Still sobbing, my sister looked up him.

Father grabbed the air with his empty hand, then blew on his fist.

I found myself believing that when he opened his hand again, the glass would be there, intact.

Father opened his hand. There was nothing in it.

He showed off his empty hand.

"There's no magic that can put something back together once it's broken."

Father had my sister go fetch another glass from the kitchen.

She brought it back with utmost care, gripping it with both hands.

"Milk, too, can't go back in the glass once it's spilled."

Father enclosed the new glass in his hands and blew on it.

My sister's sobbing continued.

Father nodded once, then opened his hands and revealed the still-empty glass.

"See? It can't go back to the way it was. Unfortunately, no magic can un-spill what's been spilt."

My sister snuffled loudly.

Father then took the empty glass out of my sister's hands and slammed it onto the nearby table.

My whole body trembled, shocked by the sound.

Father blew on the glass, then slowly took his hand away.

My eyes grew wide.

For instead of milk, the glass was filled to the brim with animal crackers.

Father picked up the glass and presented it to my sister with a flourish, saying, "Please enjoy, Madame."

But my sister just burst into tears again, even louder than before, her face turning bright red. So, I took the glass myself and began eating the animal crackers one by one. Were they shaped like cows? Birds? Some other animal? I no longer recall.

For her part, Mother never held the stone to her ear again in my sister's presence, or even mine.

In the middle of the night, I whispered to my sister.

"Can you hear it?

"Pssst, hey—can you hear it?"

I whispered again and again.

But no answer came.

Outside our window, the rain stopped.

I figured she might be asleep. But as soon as I had the thought, I heard a small voice below me.

"Sis?"

I froze in my bed, staring into the darkness.

"Can we stop that kid stuff? It's stupid."

I remained frozen, saying nothing in reply.

My sister continued.

"The 'voice of radiation'—it's so dumb. There's no way you can hear the voice of something like that."

Counting the knots in the wood grain in the ceiling above me, I couldn't understand what my sister was saying.

After all, she was the one who'd told me about it!

The room had been dark, and I couldn't tell, listening to her from the bunk below me, if she'd been smiling or distraught as she said it, but she'd said it, her voice clear and sure.

Mother's listening to the voice of radiation.

The voice in the stone—it was coming from that horrible thing called radiation?

That's what Mother's been listening to?

I couldn't believe it.

I couldn't believe Mother would listen to such a horrible thing.

It had to be some kind of mistake.

My eyes had felt clear and bright; I hadn't felt sleepy at all.

Out there in the darkness beyond the window, the fig tree had been growing, leaves sprouting vibrantly from its branches.

I found myself thinking the same thought again and again.

Our mother was trying so hard to hear the voice of something so horrible?

Such a thing couldn't be true.

It just couldn't.

I shut my eyes tight.

All I could hear was my sister's soft breathing as she slept.

We would never speak of hearing the voice again.

Eventually, the television stopped talking about radioactivity falling from the sky as well.

The rain stopped.

It's so easy to forget about things if you can't see them.

My sister began speaking to our mother once more.

Though she never wore her lace clothing again.

I—*we*—forgot everything. Or at least seemed to.

It was as if nothing had ever happened.

Our mother finally finished that lace she'd been working on. It was so big it ended up draped over our dining room table.

LOOKING DOWN AT the iPad resting on my knees, I watched the glowing ball of light blink slowly from where it remained, unmoving, right next to the Olympic Stadium.

The taxi exited the tunnel and the Imperial Palace grounds spread out green as a forest beside us.

The sun was just beginning to descend, deepening and lengthening the shadows as I watched.

The taxi encountered branching roads one after another and would make each choice so smoothly, shifting lanes and proceeding toward its goal.

I'd never been one to balk at putting effort into things.

I'd worked hard, given my all.

If not left, then right. If not right, then left.

Follow the white arrow.

There had been so many white arrows.

If not left, then right. If not right, then left.

But somehow, after all that effort, I'd lost my way.

Where did I go wrong? How far back would I have to go to get back on the right track?

There's no magic that can put something back together once it's broken.

No magic can un-spill what's been spilt.

MY FATHER WAS hospitalized the first summer after I started high school.

Even in the hospital, that watch with its glowing green face never left his wrist.

There in his private room, the bulky television set next to his bed was showing the Barcelona Olympics Opening Ceremony.

Jets danced across the pale sky, drawing the five Olympic rings in colored smoke behind them.

Watching this, Father turned to us and said,

"Objects fall.

"Lights go out.

"People die.

"It's just the way things are—no sense fighting it."

He looked up, and then blew into the space above him.

I stared, eyes wide, waiting for something to appear.

What kind of magic could he have done?

But nothing appeared.

I might have just been fooled by his labored breathing.

On the television, commentators were explaining with some passion how Barcelona had tried once before to host the Olympics but had lost out, and that these Olympics, fifty-six years later, represented a sweet vindication for Spain.

They were talking about the 1936 Berlin Olympics.

They were almost held in Barcelona.

But in the end, they weren't.

The sacred fire had been carried via torch relay to Berlin.

Spain boycotted the Berlin Olympics, and even planned to host their own independent games in defiance of the Nazis. But the Spanish Civil War aborted these plans as well.

After that, Spain, under the Franco dictatorship, tried again, putting forth Madrid this time as host city. But it lost out to Germany once more, as those were what became the Munich Olympics.

The commentator was wrapping up his remarks.

And so, the Olympics will finally open here in Spain, in the very stadium once built to host the independent Barcelona Games!

I looked down at my father lying in his hospital bed, grinding my teeth at his words.

Wasn't all of human history powered by the desire to do the impossible, to go against "the way things are"?

Isn't that why we humans strove to fly?

Why we strove to capture a light that would never go out?

So that we would never again have to be afraid of the dark, be afraid of death?

And even if everything went wrong,

surely some miracle would occur,

would grant our wish,

would save us in the end.

However much money we had, would it be enough?

I prayed.

However much I had to, I would pray.

My sister was standing next to me in her junior high school uniform.

"So stupid!" she murmured through gritted teeth.

Our mother was crying silently.

The relay runner used the torch in his hand to pass the sacred flame to an arrow.

The arrow drew a straight burning line through the night sky.

It flew toward the great cauldron that stood beside the clock tower. As soon as the tiny fire in the sky began to descend, the great fire in the cauldron burst upward.

No miracle arrived to save my father.

He passed away before the Barcelona Olympics ended.

His gravestone was a great chunk of granite he'd chosen himself.

And so, we were left with only the shiny black stone to hold in his place.

I descended into a hole filled with endless darkness.

Searching for light.

Always more light.

THE TAXI PASSED the sign for the exit to the stadium and almost immediately became snarled in traffic, slowing down more and more until finally coming to a stop. Trains appeared to our right, running past us as we waited.

I began to hear faint music coming from the monitor in front me—the one I thought I'd turned off.

It was the Big Band sound.

It started softly, then built to a crescendo.

"Sunrise Serenade."

Music by Frankie Carle, lyrics by Jack Lawrence.

Glenn Miller and His Orchestra was playing it.

The Frankie Carle Orchestra version had been released earlier by the U.S. War Department as part of the "V-Disc" program, dropped by parachute along with phonographs for American soldiers stationed all around the world.

I looked at the black screen in front of me and saw only myself.

I shook my head as if refusing the image and rubbed my eyes.

I noticed a small digital clock keeping time on one side of the screen.

5:19

05:29:45 July 16, 1945

The world's first nuclear bomb detonation took place at exactly 45 seconds past 5:29 in the morning.

From the moment I realized it, I couldn't rid myself of the thought.

05:29:45

Was that when the terrorist attack would happen?

It's evening, not the morning, but something may be planned anyway to coincide with the time—5:29 p.m.—and with the Olympics Opening Ceremony.

I took sunblock out of my bag and began to apply it to my face with trembling fingers.

The countdown had begun.

Only ten minutes left until 5:29.

I grabbed the door handle and tried to open the taxi door. But there was an automatic lock, and no matter how I pushed or pulled, it wouldn't budge.

The driver, startled, turned around in his seat.

"Ma'am? What are you doing?"

I tried to shout that I was getting out, but the words didn't come. I ended up growling inarticulately at him instead.

"I'm sorry, but I can't let you get out here, this is a high-speed expressway."

Irritated, I kept wrestling with the door handle.

"Ma'am—this is a high-speed expressway. Ma'am!"

The driver kept repeating this, his voice tight with anxiety.

I gripped my broken silver umbrella with one hand and used the other to fish some ¥10,000 bills from my bag and throw them in the driver's general direction.

The money floated in space.

I took every bill I had and threw them in the air.

The driver probably thought they were contaminated by radioactivity.

He cried out in alarm and shrank back in his seat. All at once, as if compelled by an unseen force, the taxi's door popped open.

Hot, sticky air flooded in, coiling around everything.

Slinging my bag over my shoulder and using my broken umbrella as a crutch, I leapt from the taxi and onto the hot asphalt of the expressway's shoulder.

As soon as I stood up straight, I had the distinct feeling that warm blood was about to flow from between my legs.

My abdomen felt heavy and my temples throbbed.

I must find Mother.

Must. Find.

I staggered forward, dragging my limbs behind me as I broke into a run down the shoulder of the expressway.

Looking back, I saw, through the haze of sunlight reflecting off the windshield, that the taxi driver was gingerly picking up one of my ¥10,000 bills between two white-gloved fingers.

I looked at the broken silver umbrella in my right hand.

It looked like the Olympic torch.

Sweat flowed in place of tears down my cheeks, down my neck, down my sides, eventually falling to the ground.

The expressway curved gently as it began to slowly descend.

My legs kept tangling with each other, my pumps threatening to slide off, as I ran down the shoulder, until I finally took first one, then the other, off my feet and threw them away. I pulled down my knee-high stockings too and stuffed them in my bag. I ran across the burning asphalt in my bare feet.

Still untucked, my white rayon blouse fluttered behind me as I ran.

Olympia. In Greece.

I had become Hestia, Goddess of the Sacred Fire.

I raised my broken silver umbrella high in the air.

My hands tingled, the bottoms of my feet were burning, nausea rose in my throat, but still I kept running as fast as I could.

I ran past all the cars lined up beside me.

Everyone gawped at me from behind their hermetically sealed windows. Some even had their phones out, filming me as I ran.

They were like people gawping at their televisions. As if they were in a completely separate place, somewhere far away. And it was from there that they watched me pass.

The road was making a sweeping curve.

At the end of it, I saw the green sign marking the exit off the expressway.

I broke into a wobbly sprint.

Sunlight shone down at an angle, illuminating the verdant leaves of the ginkgoes lining Gaien Avenue.

The avenue was also lined with police on traffic duty. Young volunteers dressed in the customary Olympic blue-and-white-checkered polo shirts dashed this way and that amid the throngs of people crowding the area around the stadium.

I ran straight into the crowd as if to cut right through them.

A family that looked to be from India shouted encouragement at me, then turned to take a group selfie as I ran past in the background. They seemed to take my barefoot dash through the crowd for some sort of performance.

Following suit, others in the crowd began to notice me, then hold up their cameras and phones to film me. Soon everyone was watching me on the screens in their hands.

Only a man dressed like a bellhop standing at the entrance of the Parliamentary Museum failed to take out a camera or phone as I passed; instead, an uncomfortable look crossed his face, and he averted his eyes.

I crossed the street against a blinking signal, using the crosswalk.

A grand view opened up before my eyes.

Rising up against the sky, there it was: the newly rebuilt Japan National Stadium, now the Olympic Stadium.

I approached the towering edifice as if helpless to resist its allure.

Crowds were forming all around the stadium.

I must find Mother.

Must.

Find.

Wild-eyed, my shoulders heaving, I cast about, searching for her.

Across from the Meiji Memorial Picture Gallery, where the ballpark had been, there was now a row of small prefab buildings set up just for the Olympics.

One of the people standing in front of them was a woman facing away from me.

She looked like Mother.

She wore a satin skirt.

Beside her was a man wearing what looked like pajamas.

There were mothers with their children.

Everywhere I looked, there were people who looked like my mother.

A SMALL SKIRMISH had broken out between a security guard and an old man at the Aoyama Gate to the stadium.

The man looked to be around eighty years old and was wearing a suit despite the heat. His grey hair was sticking up from his head as he raised his voice in anger.

"You think I've gone gaga? I'm no Trinity! Oh, you're *sorry*? You think that makes it better? You need to learn some respect! I have a ticket!"

The old man shoved the ticket in his hand under the guard's nose.

"So you can stop making a fool of me! You know how much this thing cost?!"

Just behind him a woman walked up and began to slide by, her gait wobbly and unsteady. Her hair was black, and she was wearing jeans—she looked no older than sixty, but I could clearly see that she was carrying a stone in her hand.

A Trinity!

My heart fairly stopped.

Not only her—there might be all sorts of Trinities gathered here!

But of course, among them were ticketholders like that old man, people who came simply to see the sacred fire themselves. There was no way to tell just by looking who was a Trinity and who was simply a spectator. After all, it wasn't even enough to search people's pockets—you'd have to search their whole bodies, every nook and orifice. Which was of course impossible.

Trinity!

Trinity!!

Trinity!!!

Terror engulfed me.

Everyone in the crowds around me—every single one of them—began to seem like Trinities, like terrorists.

I tucked my umbrella under my arm and took the iPad out of my bag. I used my trembling fingers to enlarge the map with its pulsing ball of light. It showed me that the source of the light should be right next to me.

I kept looking back and forth between the iPad screen and my surroundings.

Where was she?

Where?!

At the edge of the expanse of asphalt where I was standing, a large, pitch-black stone monument had been erected in the shade of a pine tree. Its placement seemed to correspond exactly with the pulsing ball of light on the map.

Wielding the iPad in one hand and my broken umbrella like a bamboo spear in the other, I leaned forward and charged toward the stone.

And then it happened, the moment I got close enough to read the inscription on the stone. My legs tangled together. I lurched forward, my body falling toward the ground. The iPad and the silver umbrella flew into the air.

I looked around as I propped myself back up from where I lay sprawling.

Had I tripped over a stone again?

But what my eyes landed on wasn't a shiny black stone—it was a shiny black smartphone.

I could clearly see the sticker plastered to its back.

DEATH BE NOT PROUD

I sat up all the way and grabbed the phone to look at it.

I could distinctly feel menstrual blood seeping from between my legs.

I need to get to a bathroom!

But it was already too late.

Blood was flooding out from my crotch.

It ran down my thighs and pooled there, staining my khaki pants vivid red.

I tried to do something about it, dabbing at the stains with my hands, but all I succeeded in doing was covering my hands with vivid red as well.

A couple passing by me noticed, the man even letting out a small cry of surprise. Other passersby began to look over as he shouted.

"That's blood! You're bleeding!"

A murmur spread through the crowd.

"Are you okay?"

People began to gather around.

"Did you stab someone? Were you stabbed?"

"I'm going to try to stop the bleeding, okay?"

My broken silver umbrella lay beside me, apparently looking like some kind of weapon.

I clutched my daughter's phone to me and looked around once more.

But my mother was nowhere to be seen.

Where was she?

Where on earth did she go?

I gathered my thoughts even as my mind fogged over.

Why would my daughter's phone, and only the phone, end up here?

Maybe my sister already found Mother. Maybe when she did, Mother dropped the phone without realizing.

But as soon as I had the thought, another one intruded.

What if she dropped it here on purpose?

What if my sister found our mother and then dropped the phone here deliberately?

So I couldn't find her myself?

Maybe my sister knew everything!

Maybe she was the one who sent Mother on her mission!

Maybe she'd been in on the whole thing from the start!

My eyes widened as I looked frantically around me, searching the area again.

What was happening?

I tried to shout but vomited instead.

My stomach was nearly empty, so all that emerged was some greenish bile.

My sister always did whatever she pleased, never thinking of anyone else!

A woman in a dress was carefully picking up the things that had fallen from my bag, scattered across the grass. A wide-shouldered man ran over and tried to use a handkerchief to staunch the flow of blood from between my thighs. I pushed his hand away while bringing my daughter's phone up to guard my face.

The phone's black screen suddenly lit up.

As if compelled by an unseen force, the phone's home screen appeared before my eyes.

For a moment, I couldn't understand what had happened.

It was a miracle.

But then I realized, and I couldn't help but laugh as I sat there staring at it.

My daughter's face resembled mine enough that the facial recognition software had unlocked the phone when I brought it to my face.

The crowd gathered around me fell back as I sat there laughing, covered in blood.

I held my daughter's phone up with one hand and brushed away the hair sticking to my sweaty forehead and cheek with the other.

I heard chimes notifying me of incoming messages. The notifications appeared on the screen as pop-ups.

You have a new message from Trinity.

You have a new message from Trinity.

You have a new message from Trinity.

Again and again, the same notification.

I couldn't believe my eyes.

It was like I was looking at my own phone.

Trinity

Trinity

Trinity

I checked the sticker on the back again and again to make sure it was my daughter's phone, not mine.

But no matter how many times I did, the fact remained: it was hers.

I grew dizzy.

My own daughter—having cybersex!

Filled with trepidation, I tapped the screen.

The yellow inverted triangle appeared, then the Trinity site's automatic log-in screen, and then the inbox.

I tapped the New Messages button with my finger.

I read what appeared and the breath stopped in my throat.

>> **Cerberus, please respond! I don't care what kind of perverted things you might want to do with me!**

Trembling, I tapped message after message.

>> **I'm touching myself now, imaging you licking my pussy**

>> **You must be especially good at that, right? With a name like Cerberus ?**

My eyes widened again.

No.

It can't be true.

All the messages I was reading were ones I'd just sent Cerberus.

It had to be some kind of mistake!

I needed it to be some kind of mistake.

I opened up her Trinity inbox to look at all her messages.

I felt the blood slowly drain from the finger I'd been using to tap the screen.

>> Hey, Cerberus, I'm touching myself right now. I'm *so* wet . . .

>> Hello Cerberus. What sort of play are you into?

>> I'm doing what you said, Cerberus—I'm walking outside right now without my panties on!

It was an endless series of messages in her inbox, all conversations with Cerberus. Cerberus, it turned out, had been carrying on not just with me but with many, many women.

Sometimes they asked him to lick them "down there," sometimes they asked him to thrust into them as hard as he could. They asked and they asked and they asked and they asked.

>> Oh, oh, I'm about to come!

>> Oh, I can't stand it anymore!

>> Come! Come inside me!

>> Oh, look at you, you're hard again already!

I couldn't believe what I was reading—I couldn't believe what was laid out so clearly right before my very eyes.

After all, this was my daughter. My own daughter!

My daughter who had emerged from my own body, who had been with me her whole life, who was supposed to be the person I knew best in all the world!

And it was this daughter who I now knew had been Cerberus all along.

I could see through the crowd of people still gathered—albeit now at a safe distance—around me that there were security guards approaching.

Blood was still flowing from between my legs.

I could feel the warm blood spreading down my thighs.

So, in short, it turns out I've been having cybersex with my own daughter all this time.

Everything before my eyes turned white, as if obliterated by a flash of light.

I picked up my broken umbrella again and swung it around in front of me.

I heard a scream.

Two security guards ran up and grabbed me from both sides.

I cried out, making sounds that refused to become words. Why were they trying to arrest me? What had I done?

After all the effort I'd made? Don't I deserve more than this?

My daughter's phone slipped from my grasp and slowly fell back onto the ground.

For some reason, I found myself thinking of uranium.

Of Uranus, the Sky God, for whom it was named. He reigned over the heavens, according to Greek myth.

He was the product of Gaia, the Earth Goddess, despite her virginity.

But once she gave birth, Gaia made love to her son.

And when mother and son—Earth and Sky—made love, the world was visited by darkness.

For this is the birth of the night.

I could see the screen still lit up on my daughter's phone, now on the ground. There were numbers on it telling the time.

5:29 p.m.

My body lost its strength and all at once, I collapsed. I sank to the earth.

17:30

ll I could hear was the sound of the siren.

Cut off from the cacophony of the outside world, I was left alone with the thudding of my heart.

I could smell the sunblock on me.

My head hurt.

I felt like I might throw up again.

The air-conditioning was turned up too high. The cold made me shiver.

Finally, I slowly opened my eyes.

I moaned.

The windows of this vehicle were covered in film, preventing me from seeing outside.

I was in an ambulance.

Had the sun already gone down?

I tried to move my hands.

My left hand felt nothing, but there seemed to be something hard gripped in my right hand.

A stone.

Perhaps I'd grabbed it as I collapsed.

I didn't know if it was the stone I'd stuffed in my bag or a different one I'd picked up from next to the monument.

Whatever the case, I brought the stone to my ear.

I closed my eyes.

I heard the voice.

There were creaking sounds all around me.

I was down in the depths, only darkness above me. The ocean's floor, where no light could reach.

My body was rocking gently.

The voice pressed in on me.

I moaned softly as intense nausea swept over me and my head exploded with pain.

I felt as if my eardrums were about to rupture, as if my heartbeat might rip me apart.

A landscape swung into view, out beyond the voice.

Two men lying in a narrow bunk bed dressed in crewmen's uniforms of grey leather.

I'm in a submarine.

The amount of breathable air decreases steadily the longer a submarine is underwater. The oxygen disappears little by little as time goes on.

As a submarine changes level, the pressure changes as well, putting stress on the eardrums.

When this submarine left Kiel Bay, it was on fire.

The snow had stopped, and all that filled the air was the smell of burning.

The bay had been touched by the flame of the Berlin Olympics, having served as the site of the yacht-racing competition. But what burned now was no sacred fire—it was the naval base, the city hall, the church of Saint Nikolai, the opera house.

The movie theater survived, and the film *Kolberg* played across its screen—blonde-haired, azure-eyed Kristina Söderbaum rushing about so vigorously in her apron-dress.

Docked in the bunker at Kiel Bay was one of the Grey Wolves that were the pride of the German army: a submarine named U-234. It too had been made by Krupp, the same company that had made the Berlin Olympic torch.

And now here we were, secreted away in the bottom of the ocean, in the bottom of this submarine.

The deep dark.

The depths of the earth.

I had been in darkness, deep within the earth.

But one day, the earth was excavated, and I was pulled out into the light of the sun.

It was Sankt Joachimsthal.

The men who excavated me—who excavated *us*—were not miners.

They were prisoners of war, brought here from France and Russia.

Flags bearing the hooked cross of Nazi Germany flew now above this town.

We were brought to a train station near the Radium Palace Hotel and loaded into a train.

But this time, the train wasn't bound for Paris, but rather the Auergesellschaft plant in Oranienburg, Germany, just outside Berlin. And what was extracted from us *accursed stones* this time was not radium, but uranium-235.

We were then packed into rectangular brown packages.

Forty-five in total, roughly twenty-five centimeters square.

The box we were packed in weighed about 560 kilograms.

This package of uranium-235 was then packed into the U-boat U-234—only one digit off.

The package rode the U-boat accompanied by two Japanese men.

One wore round spectacles; this was Naval Technical Officer Lieutenant Colonel Genzō Shōji. The other one, the slightly younger of the two, was Naval Technical Officer Lieutenant Colonel Hideo Tomonaga. Lt. Col. Tomonaga could often be heard humming Schumann's "Träumerei" to himself.

Träumerei. Daydream.

Supervising the Japanese officers was the monocled Luftwaffe General der Flieger Ulrich Kessler. He'd been implicated in a recent assassination attempt on Hitler, so this mission was part of a plan to flee for his life. He was anxious to get on board and start the journey.

His wish was granted soon enough.

The U-boat left the shore and headed out into the ocean.

The surface of the ocean was littered with mines and the sky above crowded with bombers, making it nearly impossible to surface.

The oxygen levels were being stretched to their limit.

The water in the toilets shone with pale light from clouds of bioluminescent sea creatures.

The U-boat headed south along the Atlantic Ocean floor.

The men were stricken with severe nausea and headaches, but they lay in their bunks as silently as possible in an effort to conserve what little oxygen they had left.

May 1, 1945.

A coded message was received in the wireless communications room.

Der Führer, Reichskanzler Hitler, is dead.

The message continued.

The 70,000 German soldiers defending Berlin have surrendered to Allied forces.

The Northern German Army has also surrendered.

Surrender.

Surrender.

Surrender.

Nazi Germany has unconditionally surrendered.

Engulfed in darkness, down in the bottom of the ocean, the men began discussing their options.

What if we were to flee straight from here to Argentina?

Surrendering to the Soviets, or the English—who knows what might happen to us?

Germany may have surrendered, but the Great Empire of Japan has not!

The two Japanese men spoke vehemently, in fluent German.

His Majesty the Emperor will continue to fight!

A living god cannot surrender.

This package must reach Japan!

Everyone is waiting for us!

If only Japan could get that package, could get that uranium, then they could make a uranium bomb—a nuclear weapon!

Rumors flew through the streets of Japan.

The nation's great scientists were busy trying to create a bomb the likes of which the world had never seen!

A matchbook-sized piece of it would be enough to bathe New York City in flames.

And in fact, a top-secret project to develop a nuclear weapon in Japan was indeed underway. A collaboration between Dr. Yoshio Nishina at the National Institute of Physical and Chemical Research and the Japanese Imperial Army called the Ni-gō Project.

The intended target for the uranium bomb was Saipan.

If Saipan was taken out, the distance to fly over Japan would be too great, and Allied bombing of the mainland would be prevented.

It would save so many lives.

This was the reasoning.

A nuclear bomb as Divine Wind.

A scientific kamikaze.

If Japan could only get its hands on it, the war would be won.

And besides, if the project failed now, the ¥20,000,000 invested in it would vanish like a popped bubble.

The men in the U-boat discussed their options.

The two Japanese men advocated continuing their journey to the Empire of Japan.

But they were outvoted—the other men chose surrender.

They wouldn't listen to the Japanese men's arguments.

They poured diesel on a pure-white bedsheet to dye it black.

This was the black flag of surrender that flew from the U-boat's periscope when it surfaced.

They chose to surrender to America.

After all, America was the vast New World. Surely preferable to surrendering to England or the Soviet Union.

As the German men prepared for surrender, the two Japanese soldiers wrote out their final testaments and then swallowed Luminal. They lay together in the same narrow bunk, dressed not in Japanese military uniforms but in the grey leather uniforms of German U-boat crewmen, their arms locked in a tight embrace, snoring unnaturally.

The U-boat surrendered to the American destroyer *Sutton*.

The two Japanese men were buried at sea, as stipulated in their testaments.

Their bodies were wrapped in spotless white canvas, along with their swords.

And then, under cover of night, they were dumped into the water.

The two bodies sank.

To the depths of the ocean floor, they sank into darkness.

The package never made it to Japan.

The nuclear weapon was never built.

Neither God nor Buddha answered their prayers.

They would not listen to them.

No Divine Wind blew.

No miracle occurred.

All that effort in vain.

Surrender.

Defeat.

But it didn't end there—not life, not history, not the world.

For this weapon that was so wished for did end up arriving in Japan—dropped on it, rather than created.

From the skies above Hiroshima.

From the skies above Nagasaki.

The nuclear bombs arrived.

I slowly opened my eyes.

6:52 p.m.

The sun was setting on another day.

CREAM-COLORED CURTAINS fluttered around me.

I found myself in a hospital bed, an IV attached to my left arm.

Clear liquid slowly formed into a drop, and then, succumbing to gravity, fell.

I heard women's voices in passing. Were they doctors or nurses? Or just visitors?

"So how did it turn out? Did we get gold? Silver?"

Were they talking about swimming? Or the long jump, or judo, or archery . . . ?

The Olympics had begun.

It seemed that while I was sleeping, I'd missed the Opening Ceremony entirely.

But I knew.

The great terrorist action had succeeded.

I looked at the ceiling.

Panels arranged in perfect order.

I smiled to myself.

In fact, my face was so rigid I could hardly move my lips, but still: I smiled.

It was so easy.

05:29:46

All you had to do is measure the circumference of that Olympic Stadium that I—*we*—surrounded.

You'd find that it was the same as that of the hole left in the earth after the first Trinity explosion.

That gaping hole ripped into the earth by the world's first nuclear bomb.

A hole filled with fluorescent green glass made of sand melted together by the heat.

That glass is now called Trinitite. But the hole was filled in right away.

But I—*we*—made it appear again, showed everyone its grandeur.

I opened my mouth and tried to laugh out loud.

Everyone, together—let's dig that hole!

BUT ALL THAT came out of my mouth was a moan.

At last, the revenge of the invisible begins.

I heard a sound.

The sound of breaking ground,

of the surface of the earth ripping open,

of excavation, of digging deeper and deeper and deeper . . .

The past—all that had been buried deep within the earth, invisible—was finally brought back to the surface, to be touched once more by the light of the sun.

But in the end, what became of me—of *us*?

U-234 surrendered and was escorted to its eventual resting place at the seaport of Portsmouth in New Hampshire, U.S.A.

The German soldiers in their Nazi uniforms filed out onto shore.

All that's known about the package is testimony telling of it setting off a Geiger counter and being sent to Robert Oppenheimer for further study. Nothing more is known about *our* destiny.

Two months later, at 5:29 a.m. on Monday, July 16, 1945, at the Trinity test site at the White Sands Proving Ground in New Mexico, the world's first nuclear bomb, the Gadget, exploded in a flash of light.

Trinity.

No one seems to recall exactly why such a place received such a name.

Was it borrowed from that of a nearby accursed mountain shunned by even the Native Americans? Or was it simply because the nuclear bomb experiment would be completed in three phases: first, the initial detonation of the Gadget; second, the dropping of Little Boy onto Hiroshima; and, finally, third, the dropping of Fat Man onto Nagasaki?

J. Robert Oppenheimer, director of the Manhattan Project, attempted, years later, to recall the reason for it, but failed to remember clearly. All he said was something to the effect of, *When I came up with the name, I'm sure I had that poem by John Donne somewhere in the back of my mind.*

The debate still rages as to whether the uranium-235 in the package recovered from the German U-boat was used in the core of the bomb dropped on Hiroshima, or if the U.S. had enough uranium by then that there was no need for it.

And so, where did *we* really end up, after everything was said and done?

Perhaps we should ask the stones.

I SLOWLY OPENED my eyes once more. My daughter was standing next to the bed looking down at me, a worried look on her face.

I looked at the lace vest she was wearing.

I looked at the pattern the yarn made, the complex matrix of it, the twisting, meandering, winding path of the threads as they looped together.

1

2

3

4

5

I counted the loops.

Finally, I understood so clearly what it meant—what that mysterious patterning had always been trying to tell me.

I could finally see, right there in front me.

I could see so clearly the person standing before my very eyes.

THREE-PERSON'D GOD

"Batter my heart, three-person'd God; for you
As yet but knock; breathe, shine, and seek to mend;
That I may rise, and stand, o'erthrow me, and bend
Your force, to break, blow, burn, and make me new."

—JOHN DONNE, *HOLY SONNET XIV* (1631)

Lately, even when it was light outside, I found I couldn't tell if it was morning or evening, if the sun was coming up or on its way back down. When I forced my eyelids apart to check, all I saw was a wide plane of sky the color of burning.

I blinked and blinked again.

Looking over from my pillow, I caught sight of a clock.

5:23

Reading the digits, I remembered so clearly.

That American-made cooling tower.

The moment criticality was achieved, overseen by scientists, right there in the little town of Tōkai in Ibaraki Prefecture.

The nuclear flame was lit. There was a parade for children.

Even as I recalled it, time marched on. The digits now read 5:24.

My mouth was so dry.

I tried to use my left hand to grab the thermos sitting on the table beside the clock.

But my hand refused to move. It sat there, lolling on the bed—I couldn't even feel it refusing to move; I couldn't even feel it exist. It was as if I had no hand at all.

But still—I was so thirsty. I wrestled my right hand over to reach for the thermos.

I somehow managed to grab it, but I couldn't figure out how to open its top. I pushed on it in different places until, suddenly, a straw-like protuberance popped up.

Slowly, carefully, I put my mouth on the plastic straw. I sucked with all my might. What filled my mouth was not water, though, but something thick and heavy, choking me. The heavy liquid dribbled from the corners of my mouth and down my chin and neck, falling from me.

My shirt became wet, sticking to my chest.

I roused myself to wipe it away and then froze, shocked.

What was this costume I was wearing?

I looked down and saw myself dressed in black silk pajamas, top and bottom. They were strangely glossy. I'd remembered myself wearing something more normal, a T-shirt or something, but when I tried to remember exactly which T-shirt it might have been, I found I couldn't recall anything clearly enough to hold onto.

I looked around.

All that was visible through the window was sky.

Where is this place? Who am I?

I seemed to have forgotten.

I felt as though I'd been sleeping for quite a long time.

Even as it also seemed like quite a long time since I woke up.

White tissue paper sticking up from the box on the round table next to the bed fluttered in the breeze from the air conditioner.

A spacious room. White flooring. White walls.

There was a single small picture hanging on the wall.

What was it?

I squinted but saw nothing.

Just silver.

I had the feeling that if I could touch it, I would remember something. I concentrated my strength into my right hand and pushed my body up with it. I tried to get out of bed. My arms and legs flailing, I found myself sliding from the bed toward the ground.

I grabbed the round table next to the bed, toppling it with me as I fell.

The plastic box atop it fell onto me.

My forehead hurt so much it felt like it was splitting open.

The too-white ceiling above me seemed to move slowly as I watched.

A moan escaped my lips.

I turned over, lying on my side.

I felt something warm and touched my hand to my head; my fingers came away slick with red. I felt a scream building within me.

Blood. It's blood. I didn't really know why, but I started wiping my forehead with my hand. I wiped again and again but to no avail, the blood just kept flowing. I wiped furiously with my hands, trying to remove it. Blood stains spread across the flooring beneath me. Still wiping, I slowly looked up.

The door to the room was opening.

A girl stood in the doorway, alone.

She looked to be around thirteen or fourteen. Golden skin, deep dark eyes, short hair. What country could she be from? Seeing me, the girl's eyes widened into saucers.

"Grandma, are you okay?"

She ran to me as she shouted her question.

She wore a tight-fitting white tank top that looked to me like something you'd wear to bed, pulled over her small breasts. As she knelt beside me, her firm, pants-less thighs emerged from beneath it, exposed.

Still, I could see as she got closer that she had lace around her middle. And I could see so clearly the message conveyed by its pattern.

The girl turned away from me, her full lips parting to allow her to scream toward the door.

"Come here! Quick!"

She turned back to me.

"Don't worry, they're coming, you're going to be all right."

Behind her, in the window, the sun continued to look as if it were both coming up and going down.

By the way, I think, *I've been meaning to ask—you keep saying Grandma, Grandma, but tell me: who is "Grandma"?*

I looked behind me to see if someone was standing there.

Grandma?

But there was no one there, no one behind me at all, and so it must be me, I'm the one she must be calling "Grandma"!

Grandma!

I looked at the girl straight on.

This girl—she's mine? And not even my daughter, but my granddaughter?

If I'm her grandma, *that means I must have given birth to either her mother or father . . .*

I narrowed my eyes at her.

"Excuse me for asking, but who are you again?"

The girl started laughing, and she pointed to the lacework wrapped around her torso.

"Grandma, look here! That's me! My moms worked my name into the lace so you wouldn't forget!"

And sure enough, when I looked again, I saw letters woven into the lace with red thread.

TRINITY

The girl spoke again, whispering to me conspiratorially.

"That's when they met, after all—that year.

"So that's what they named me."

Listening to her, I asked, "So that's the name your mother and father gave you?"

The girl shook her head and laughed again, baring her bright white teeth in her amusement.

"Not exactly. My *mothers* gave it to me."

The girl wiped the blood that dripped still from my forehead.

Moms.

Mothers.

I turned her words over in my mind, and my eyes fixed upon her hand, the one that wasn't using the tissue to wipe me clean.

There was a lump of stone in it.

Her palm was too white, and the shiny stone too black against it.

The girl gripped me around the waist, using the waistband of my pajama bottoms to hoist me up.

About halfway to standing, I realized that the crotch of my pajamas was dark and wet.

Which of my hundreds of eggs was this?

Clinging to the girl, I pulled myself to my feet.

My fingers touched the lace around her belly.

1, 2, 3, 4, 5

1, 2, 3, 4, 5

I traced the loops. Like a countdown in reverse.

Again and again, I reversed the countdown.

1, 2, 3, 4, 5

1

2

3

4

5

A thread becomes a loop, then hooks to another loop, and then another, and forms a pattern.

But the pattern I'd been weaving went wrong somewhere, I must have made a mistake along the way.

I moved my body as if dragging it.

Everything around me grew dark.

I must turn on the light!

"Hey, Siri!"

I turned, cried out to a machine and then fell, swallowed by the dark.

Darkness.

I HEARD THE sound of a door opening and shutting.

I heard the sound of footsteps loudly approaching.

This must be the women that girl called her "moms."

I heard them talking to each other in hushed tones.

One of the women leaned close to my ear and shouted.

"Mom, are you okay?!"

She called me Mom—does that mean this is my daughter's voice?

"Mom!"

A different woman's voice this time, calling me Mom as well. Did I have two daughters?

One of them laughed a little.

"She's always like this."

The other woman began to laugh along with her.

"Anyway. We can watch the Olympics another time."

I heard the women walking hurriedly around my bed.

"I wonder if they've stopped traffic for the torch relay already? Though I guess that won't matter much for an ambulance . . ."

The sound of footsteps receded, grew distant.

Quiet returned to the room.

I heard the girl whisper in my ear.

"Can you hear it?"

My right hand held a stone.

I slowly brought it to my ear.

I answered, my voice clear at last.

"I can.

"I can hear it."

I slowly opened my eyes.

I could see every memory there was to see, no matter how distant, more clearly now than ever before.

The sky was vivid red.

The color of burning.

REFERENCES

NON-JAPANESE

Alexievich, Svetlana. *Chernobyl Prayer: A Chronicle of the Future.* Translated by Anna Gunin and Arch Tait. London: Penguin Modern Classics, 2017.

Bird, Kai, and Martin J. Sherwin. *American Prometheus: The Triumph and Tragedy of J. Robert Oppenheimer.* New York: Vintage, 2006.

Clark, Claudia. *Radium Girls: Women and Industrial Health Reform, 1910–1935.* Chapel Hill: The University of North Carolina Press, 1997.

Curie, Eve. *Madame Curie.* Translated by Vincent Sheean. New York: Doubleday, 1938.

Doyle, Sir Arthur Conan. *The Sign of the Four,* in *The Complete Sherlock Holmes.* New York: Race Point Publishing, 2013.

Goethe, Johann Wolfgang von. *Letters from Goethe.* Translated by Dr. M. von Herzfeld and C. Melvil Sym. Edinburgh: Edinburgh University Press, 1957.

———. *Faust: A Tragedy.* Translated by Martin Greenberg. New Haven: Yale University Press, 2014.

Goldsmith, Barbara. *Obsessive Genius: The Inner World of Marie Curie.* New York: W. W. Norton, 2005.

Hedin, Sven. "Olympia-Tokyo." *Journal of Olympic History* 13, no. 2 (May/June 2005): 50–56.

Hersey, John. *Hiroshima.* New York: Vintage Books, 1989.

Hoffman, Klaus. *Otto Hahn: Achievement and Responsibility*. Translated by J. Michael Cole. New York: Springer, 2001.

Isaacson, Walter. *Einstein: His Life and Universe*. New York: Simon & Schuster, 2007.

International Olympic Committee. *Report of the Organizing Committee on Its Work for the XIIth Olympic Games of 1940 in Tokyo Until the Relinquishment*. Berlin: Wilhelm Limpert, 1940.

Jungk, Robert. Translated by James Cleugh. *Brighter than a Thousand Suns: A Personal History of the Atomic Scientists*. Boston: Mariner Books, 1970.

Levi, Primo. *If This is a Man*. Translated by Stuart Woolf. New York: The Orion Press, 1959.

Miller, Richard L. *Under the Cloud: The Decades of Nuclear Testing*. Woodlands, TX: Two-Sixty Press, 1991.

Organisationskomitee für die XI Olympiade Berlin 1936 E. V. *The XIth Olympic Games Berlin, 1936: Official Report*. Lausanne: IOC, 1937.

Sime, Ruth Lewin. *Lise Meitner: A Life in Physics*. Berkeley: University of California Press, 1997.

Streshinsky, Shirley, and Patricia Klaus. *An Atomic Love Story: The Extraordinary Women in Robert Oppenheimer's Life*. New York: Turner, 2013.

Veselovský, František, Petr Ondruš, and Jiří Komínek. "History of the Jáchymov (Joachimsthal) Ore District [*Historie jáchymovského rudního revíru* (Czech summary)]." *Journal of the Czech Geological Society* 42, no. 4 (1997): 127–132.

Zoellner, Tom. *Uranium: War, Energy, and the Rock That Shaped the World*. New York: Viking Penguin, 2009.

JAPANESE

Daigo fukuryū-maru heiwa kyōkai. *Daigo fukuryū-maru wa kōkaichū: bikini suibaku hisai jiken to hibaku gyosen 60-nen no kiroku* [The Voyage of the *Lucky Dragon No. 5* Continues: A Sixty-Year Record of the Fishermen Affected by the Bikini Atoll Hydrogen Bomb Detonation]. Tokyo: Daigo Fukuryū-maru heiwa kyōkai, 2014.

Hashimoto, Kazuo. *Maboroshi no tōkyo orinpikku: 1940-nen taikai shōchi kara henjō made* [The Tokyo Olympics That Never Were: The 1940 Olympics, from Invitation to Relinquishment]. Tokyo: Kōdansha gakujutsu bunko, 2014.

Hosaka, Masayasu. *Nihon no genpatsu: sono kaihatsu to zasetsu no michinori* [Nuclear Japan: The Road from Development to Failure]. Tokyo: Shinchōsha, 2012.

Ikeuchi, Osamu. *Gēte-san konbanwa* [Good Evening, Goethe]. Tokyo: Shūeisha bunko, 2005.

Ishikawa-machi kyōiku iinkai. *Pegumataito no kioku: Ishikawa no kigenso kōbutsu to "ni-gō kenkyū" no kakawari* [Memories of Pegmatite: The Relation between Rare Earth Minerals in Ishikawa and the "Ni-go Project"]. Ishikawa: Fukushima-ken ishikawa-machi rekishi minzoku shiryōkan, 2013.

Kainuma, Hiroshi. *Fukushima daiichi genpatsu hairo zukan* [An Illustrated Guide to the Decommissioning of the Fukushima Daiichi Nuclear Power Plant]. Tokyo: Ōta shuppan, 2016.

———. *"Fukushima"-ron: genshiryoku-mura wa naze umareta no ka* [On "Fukushima": What Led to the Creation of the Nuclear Village?]. Tokyo: Seidosha, 2011.

Kanō, Mikiyo. *Hiroshima to fukushima no aida: jendā no shiten kara* [Between Hiroshima and Fukushima: From the Perspective of Gender]. Tokyo: Impact shuppankai, 2013.

Kawashima, Keiko. *Marī kyurī no chōsen: kagaku, jendā, sensō* [The Challenge of Marie Curie: Science, Gender, War]. Tokyo: Transview, 2010.

"Kigen ni-sen roppyaku nen no onnatachi" [The Women of the 2600th Anniversary of the Founding of Japan]. *Jūgoshi nōto: fukkan 3-gō, tsūkan 7-gō*. Tokyo: Onna-tachi no ima o tou kai, 1982.

Ministry of the Environment (Japan). *Fukushima daiichi genshiryoku kankyo hyōbansho* [Fukushima Daiichi Nuclear Power Plant Environmental Report]. 1995–1996.

Nakao, Maika. *Kaku no yūwaku: senzen nihon no kagaku bunka to "genshiryoku yūtopia" no shutsugen* [The Allure of the Nuclear: The Culture of Science in Prewar Japan and the Emergence of the "Nuclear Utopia"]. Tokyo: Keisō shobō, 2015.

———. *Kagakusha to mahō-tsukai no deshi: kagaku to hikagaku no kyokai* [The Scientist and the Sorcerer's Apprentice: The Border Between the Scientific and Unscientific]. Tokyo: Seidosha, 2019.

Yoshimura, Akira. *Shinkai no shisha* [Messenger from the Deep Sea]. Tokyo: Bunshun bunko, 2011.

OTHER MEDIA

The following films are referred to either directly or indirectly in the text: Leni Reifensthal's *Olympia* (1938), Carole Langer's *Radium City* (1987), the documentary *Visions of Eight* (1973), and the Japanese documentary *Dokyumentarii eizō: U-bōto no isho (The U-Boat's Testament)*, released by NHK Productions in 1970.

The 2020 Olympic "folk song" ("Tōkyō gorin ondo") that appears on page 29 is a song and accompanying dance created by the Tokyo Organizing Committee of the Olympic and Paralympic Games in anticipation of the 2020 Tokyo Olympics. The official lyrics are partially quoted in Kobayashi's Japanese text, and the translation that appears in English is original to Brian Bergstrom.

ACKNOWLEDGMENTS

I am filled with gratitude on the occasion of the first of my books being published in English. Above all, I must thank my translator, Brian Bergstrom, who has been reading my work with such deep understanding over the years and producing such wonderful translations of it. I must also thank the various people who helped bring about this productive relationship: Professors Saeko Kimura, Takayuki Tatsumi, and Livia Monnet. Further thanks must also go to Lisette Verhagen at Peters, Fraser, and Dunlop for supporting this book with such passion as it found its way to publication. This book would not be coming out in English at all if it weren't for you. Thanks, too, must be given to the curator Hikotaro Kanehira, the translator Alison Watts and my friend Alicia Kirby. And of course, I must also thank Danny Vazquez and everyone else at Astra House who has worked so hard to make the English edition of *Trinity, Trinity, Trinity* as wonderfully realized as it is. In Japan, I must gratefully acknowledge Shūeisha, who published the Japanese edition back in October 2019, and the museums who exhibited the works leading up to its writing: The National Art Center, Tokyo, and the Yutaka Kikutake Gallery. And to my mentors and teachers, my family, and my friends both inside and outside Japan who have supported me so much as this novel was being written and now as it is coming out in English: thank you, for everything.

ACKNOWLEDGMENTS

The Tokyo Olympics have now actually taken place, albeit a year late, the eleventh spring since the Fukushima Dai-ichi nuclear disaster is upon us, and soon it will be the seventy-seventh summer since the world witnessed the bright flash of the very first nuclear bomb. At this time, I must acknowledge each and every person who has taken this book in their hands and read it. Thank you, from the bottom of my heart.

Erika Kobayashi
March 2022

ABOUT THE AUTHOR

PHOTO BY MIE MORIMOTO

Erika Kobayashi is a novelist and visual artist based in Tokyo. In her visual art as in her writing, she explores the effects of Japan's history of nuclear power and radiation. Her novel *Breakfast with Madame Curie*, published in 2014 by Shueisha, was shortlisted for both the Mishima and Akutagawa Prizes. She was awarded the 7th Tekken Heterotopia Literary Prize in 2020 for *Trinity, Trinity, Trinity*, her second novel and first to be published in English.

ABOUT THE TRANSLATOR

Brian Bergstrom is a lecturer and translator who has lived in Chicago, Kyoto, and Yokohama. His writing and translations have appeared in publications including *Granta, Aperture, Lit Hub, Mechademia, Japan Forum, positions: asia critique,* and *The Penguin Book of Japanese Short Stories.* He is the editor and principal translator of *We, the Children of Cats* by Tomoyuki Hoshino (PM Press), which was longlisted for the 2013 Best Translated Book Award. He is currently based in Montréal, Canada.